RANDOM SURVIVAL

THE ROAD BOOK 5
SLICER

Ray Wenck
Glory Days Press
Columbus, Ohio

Copyright © 2022 by Ray Wenck 2nd Edition

All rights reserved. No part of this publication may be reproduced, distributed or transmitted in any form or by any means, without prior written permission.

Glory Days Press
Columbus, Ohio

Publisher's Note: This is a work of fiction. Names, characters, places, and incidents are a product of the author's imagination. Locales and public names are sometimes used for atmospheric purposes. Any resemblance to actual people, living or dead, or to businesses, companies, events, institutions, or locales is completely coincidental.

Book Layout © 2016 BookDesignTemplates.com
Cover Design by Mibl Art
Slicer/ Ray Wenck. – 1st edition

ISBN: 979-8-9858820-5-6

Ray Wenck

Dedication
To Jeremy. I couldn't be prouder.

Ray Wenck

Author's Notes

I find that the more I write in this series, the more I want to write. With the introduction of a new character, Slicer, the ever-expanding Random Survival universe takes a new direction. Subsequent stories will add more new players and delve deeper into the mystery of the pandemic.

Although there are no current plans for the two series to connect, it may occur down the road (no pun intended, yet fitting nonetheless) as The Road series catches up in the timeline. As fast as the stories are coming to me, who knows. That may happen but at the end of the year. But, hey, no spoilers. If you want to know more and be ahead of other readers, join my Facebook group, Ray's Ravenous Readers. They always get the heads up first, plus a lot of bonus material.

I'd like to thank my Beta readers once more for their efforts, as well as editor/author Steve Wilhelm. You can find Steve's works here:

https://www.amazon.com/Steve-Wilhelm/e/B006LGP4QC/ref=aufs_dp_fta_dsk

Lastly, thank you, readers, for all your continued support as I bring you one strange story after another.

If you are a first-time reader, you can find other titles at raywenck.com. Sign up for the newsletter to keep informed about new releases and book signings.

As always, read all you want ... I'll write more.

Ray

Ray Wenck

SLICER

Chapter One

 Jerome Smart rode his Indian Chieftain Elite motorcycle slowly down West 37th street in Chicago, searching for anyone alive. It was still the early days of the pandemic that was killing people randomly. This was his sixth day of prowling the streets. True, he had seen people on the streets or hiding behind their curtains in their homes, but in a city this size, there should be survivors. A lot of survivors. The problem was connecting with them.
 Most kept to themselves, coming outside only, when necessary, which meant in need of food, water, or medical assistance. He understood why. They feared catching the disease or being mugged by the ever-increasing number of small gangs patrolling the streets looking for easy scores. Many still didn't understand that money, gold, and jewels no longer held value. Instead, they should be stock piling food, water, medicine, and ammunition like he'd been doing over the past few days. Once he was sure the virus was deadly and that normal life was not returning anytime soon, he knew it was time to prepare for whatever future was still left to him.

He drove with caution. Though the sound of his bike drove the more timid indoors or into the shadows, the bolder survivors or gangs were drawn to the roar. He welcomed them—the street predators—the toughs who got their bravery from running with a pack. Few were bold enough to take Jerome on alone. In truth, though he didn't seek altercations, he was happy when they came. The more predators he could eliminate, the better chance others might survive.

One day he would run into someone who was his match and take him down, but it wasn't today. Confidence wasn't the best armor against a bullet. So, he rode with self-assurance. His black eyes were ever moving, scanning the shadows, surrounding areas, and beyond.

He wore his heavy, black leather riding jacket and a balaclava covering his head and face. Though he had helmets, he rarely wore one. Jerome never rode after dark. He was confident, not stupid. There were no longer streetlights or ambient light from stores or houses. You couldn't defend against what you couldn't see. At night he stayed in his apartment, with his door and windows barred and barricaded and his considerable arsenal ready should any threats come calling.

He had not found many to challenge him today and had only made three stops to collect needed supplies. One was a corner grocery that hadn't been completely stripped yet, scoring twelve assorted canned goods. Another was a gas station where he hauled away three bags of snack foods, batteries, and assorted bottles of medications from aspirin to anti-bacterial creams. The last stop had been at a bar he frequented. The booze and beer had been picked clean save for one bottle of white wine, a Sauvignon

Blanc. He smiled when he saw it knowing who would enjoy the vintage. He didn't drink, so the lack of alcohol in the bar didn't matter to him. He wasn't there for alcohol. Instead, the owner, Junior Gipson, was a friend of his. Since he buried him two days ago, yet another victim of the plague, he knew he wouldn't mind Jerome taking a few things.

He skipped the bar and went into the office near the back of the building. The door had been broken down and the room ransacked, but the intruders wanted booze and Junior didn't keep his stock in the office. He did, however, keep items of more value in today's market.

Jerome yanked the metal four-drawer file cabinet away from the wall. With one of the many knives he secreted around his body, he pried the three-foot square panel off the wall revealing the wall safe. Ever observant, Jerome had seen where Junior had written the combination as well as what was stored inside the safe. It took longer than he wanted to locate the small sticky note amidst the mess but only seconds to open the safe. Inside were stacks of twenty-dollar bills, two pounds of cocaine, three handguns of various calibers, and a sawed-off shotgun, the prize he came for.

He fished out all the guns, not wanting them to fall into hands that might one day turn them against him. He also fished out four boxes of shotgun shells and a box each of rounds for the three handguns. It was a good haul.

He got a feel for the shotgun. Its shorter barrel and pistol grip made it a perfect weapon for the bike. It could be fired with one hand while he continued to ride. He remembered as a boy watching old black and white reruns of a western where the lead character had one strapped to his leg in a special holster that allowed the weapon to be swung outward without having to draw it. He'd have to see about making one that allowed quick and easy access while on the bike.

He pushed the file cabinet back into place without replacing the panel and exited through the rear door. In the alley behind the bar, he found two young men rifling through the bags on his bike. Jerome's hand went to the back of his shirt collar. As the two men whirled on Jerome, he saw one had his hands full of his day's finds while the other held a small-caliber gun.

In one fluid motion and without hesitation, he pulled and threw the knife he kept in a sheath in a specially made harness strapped to his back. The blade flew true, striking the gunman in the chest. His gun discharged into the back of the bar. He staggered back, looked at his friend in disbelief, and fell on his butt, the gun clattering to the ground.

Jerome already had the second knife from behind his neck in throwing position. As the downed man's partner shifted his shocked gaze back his way, Jerome said, "Two choices, drop my stuff or die like your friend."

The man eyed the fallen gun. Jerome could see him tense with anger.

"Foolish choice."

The man ignored him. He held the bag of cans up as a shield as he lunged over his friend. By the time he had his fingers around the gun, the blade was whirling through the air. It embedded in the back of the man's head. He stood erect, the gun dangling from his fingers. He walked in a circle, unaware that he was dead. Not quite, but soon. A look of confusion filled his face as if trying to remember something important.

Jerome moved behind him, palmed the blade in deeper, causing the man to spasm, then twisted and withdrew the blade. The man dropped. He yanked the knife from the first man, who was still in disbelief over his fate, then gathered and repacked his things. He got on his bike and rode back to his apartment.

He hated killing the men. If they had left his things alone, he would have let them walk away. They weren't predators, just lazy. He judged they had been stealing since they were old enough to know the difference between honest work and stealing. They didn't know any different. It no longer mattered.

The ride was only fifteen minutes. He lived on the second floor of a three-story apartment complex. The units were functional, just short of being nice. He had been fortunate when he got out of the military to find one at this price. Now rent was no longer a concern.

He had checked on his neighbors. Only four responded to his knocks. Over the past few days, he had taken to breaking into the non-responding units taking items on his list of importance and finding a multitude of bodies. Eventually, he'd either have to do something about the bodies, or the smell and rats would drive him away.

Because of security concerns in the changing neighborhood, the landlord had equipped the outer doors with locks and given the residents keys. That served him well now. With only a few others in the building, the only way to get inside was to break out a window which would give him warning of an intruder. He used his key and wheeled his bike inside.

The elevator had stopped working two days ago. Electricity was down, but he was fine with that. He pried open the elevator doors, wedged the lesser of his two combat knives, the one he termed the utility knife into the gap at the top of the door to hold it open, and rolled the bike inside. He pulled the blade out and the door slid closed. Then he hiked up the stairs to his room.

At his door, he checked the hall for potential threats, then set his collected goods down. Whoever had lived in the apartment before him had been paranoid and paid to have a second deadbolt lock installed. Yesterday, he added a third. Did that make him paranoid as well? No, he thought, just careful. The locks were at three different heights, with the lowest three feet from the floor. Once all three were disengaged, he opened the doorknob lock, checked the hallway again, and finally gathered his items and stepped inside.

After stowing his new finds, he eyed the bottle of wine and smiled. He knew she'd be there but wished she weren't. Today he would work harder to convince her not to come back.

Chapter Two

Cynthia pressed up on her toes and held the position for several seconds as she gazed out the window. As she lowered to first position, she released a sigh. She had hoped things weren't as dire as they appeared and that even though her dance students hadn't shown up in the last three days, it was only a minor setback, and they would be there today. Deep inside, she knew they would never come again, however, if even one came, she wanted to be there for them. Now it was time to face the truth. The dance school that she had worked so hard to open and keep solvent was done.

The petite, dark-haired woman of indiscernible age rose onto her toes again, then slid one foot up her opposite leg to her knee, did a slow, graceful turn still balancing on one toe shoe, then slid into a deep bow sliding her leg along the floor behind her, her final curtain call.

Her husband Kenneth had been right. She should never have come. She didn't blame him for worrying. She was there alone, but he didn't understand how important this was to the children she worked with—to her. He told her one more day, and she had agreed. With sadness she gazed around the room, knowing she may never return. Did she strip and pack it all up? No. Someday it would open again, most likely without her, but whoever took it over at least they'd be ready.

She glided more than walked across the floor, her slim, graceful body held erect and proud. She had done good work here in the year she had been open, serving nearly a hundred underprivileged children. Many could not afford the lessons, but she took them in any way. Anyone who wanted to learn how to and about dance was accepted. Payment was something that could be worked out later, a time that mostly never came. It didn't matter though. Cynthia never turned away the students who wanted to be there.

She had worked a deal with the landlord of the small apartment complex to turn one of the lower units into a studio. He had been very understanding about late or incomplete rent payments. For a landlord, he had a big, kind heart. Hers was one of four businesses opened on the first floor. The others had ceased operation days ago.

It was time to call Kenneth to get her. Though electricity and water had stopped running, cell service was still in operation, at least for now. As she moved toward the cabinet, she locked her wrap and purse in, and the door opened. For an instant, her heart fluttered with the hope that a student had come. However, what stepped through the door was not someone yearning to learn and grow but three men more intent on destruction.

Two black men and one white strolled in and surveyed the room. The taller of the two black men, a rugged-looking hard-eyed man, swept his gaze up and down her body, then said, "Lady, we know you must have some good stuff in here. Give it up, and you don't get hurt."

The white man moved left, rummaging through cabinets. A line of low units stretched in front of the door for the students to place their belongings before class started. Nothing of value would be found there. The shorter black man with a tall Afro that swayed when he moved, opened her coat closet.

"No," she said and made a move to stop him.

The tall man grabbed her arms and swung her back into the room. Her superb training and conditioning kept her from sprawling on the floor. She whirled on him and eyed the man with fear and hatred.

"Be nice. Can't be anything in there so important to get yourself hurt."

"Take the money, take anything else but leave my purse and my cell phone."

The shorter black man said, "We take what we want. You just be happy we don't take you. Course, if you still here later, we may change our minds."

He grabbed the purse and started for the door. Cynthia could not allow him to leave. The items in her purse were irreplaceable. Her wallet contained photos of her children and grandchildren. She had no other copies. As she reached the door, her mild-mannered demeanor vanished, and all she knew was rage.

Without thought about what might happen, she raced toward the row of cabinets. In one graceful move, she placed a hand on the countertop, swung her legs over like a gymnast, and drove them into the man's side. He slammed into the wall, stunned. She had moved with such smooth speed neither of the other two men had time to react.

Cynthia landed lightly, scooped up her purse, and darted toward the white man. He reached to grab her, but she ducked, swept her leg along the floor, and took the man's legs out from under him. He lifted off the floor and fell hard with a thud and cry of pain. She was up and moving before the man hit. With the men at the door, she had two options. Head for the windows, which were small and locked, or go into the bathroom, shut the door, and hope they gave up before they got in. She opted for the latter.

To reach the bathroom she had to cut back across the room. The leader was quicker than she hoped and dove at her. His superior length and weight were enough to bear her down. She clutched the purse tightly to her chest and kept it pinned beneath her. The tall man climbed onto her back and tried to yank the bag free.

She held out until the other two men arrived and began striking her. Still, she struggled even as the pain mounted, and her bravado faltered. As she lost control of the purse, she screamed, "No, give it back." Tears flowed freely as she struggled to get out from under the man. He placed a large palm on the back of her head and pressed her face into the floor. Now under his control, she feared what might come next.

The shorter black man who had her purse fell suddenly three feet from him. His agonized eyes locked with hers as he tried to speak. Fear etched deeply into his face as he struggled to hold back the blood spurting from his sliced throat.

Shocked by the sudden gore, the man holding her down looked up, releasing the pressure on Cynthia's head. She squirmed and managed to shift her head to the side to see two sets of legs doing a freestyle dance routine. Then one man fell, the white man, hitting the floor, making no effort to stop his fall. As he bounced, she caught sight of a knife rammed up under his chin, through his mouth, and beyond. His eyes watered then the color faded.

The weight was lifted from her back. Cynthia rolled, scrambled to her feet, and snatched up her fallen purse. As she gathered the upended contents, she glanced up to see two black men in hand-to-hand combat. The taller man rotated away from her, putting his opponent's back to her. She had no idea who her savior was but was extremely grateful.

The taller man landed a solid punch to the other man's face. The blow staggered him a bit. As they danced around each other, the tall man came close. With his back to her, she snapped a kick into the back of a knee, and his leg buckled. She rolled out of the way as the other man pressed the advantage. With a series of vicious punches and a sidekick, the taller man went down. As he tried to rise, the second man pulled a knife from someplace unseen and rammed it into the man like a piston until the tall man stopped moving.

Now, unsure if she had been rescued or just moved into more trouble, she stood and hurried toward the bathroom. Then she heard the gasping breath. "Cynthia." Surprised to hear her name called, she looked back over her shoulder as she continued to move away. The lone man standing had his hands on his knees, sucking air harshly. Recognition hit and she turned. "Jerome? Is that you?" The medium-height, well-built black man winked at her.

Before he could answer, she rushed forward and embraced him. She held him for a moment, then stepped back, realizing he was still struggling for air. "Are you alright?"

He stretched, sucked in a deep breath, and said, "Yeah. Guess I'm a little out of shape."

Cynthia smiled. "I told you, you should have joined one of my classes. I would have had you in shape in no time."

"Guess you were right," he said, breathing easier. He retrieved and cleaned his knives.

"Jerome, thank you for rescuing me."

"Not a problem. Well, maybe a slight problem. I did try to warn you about coming here anymore. It's too dangerous for you here. Tell your husband to come get you. I'll stay with you until he arrives."

"I was doing just that when these men came into the studio." She looked at the mess. "Help me remove them from my studio, please." She could see he had no interest in doing so but bent to grab two feet.

"I'll do this. You call your husband."

Cynthia smiled. "Thank you, Jerome."

Chapter Three

After disposing the bodies on the far side of the parking lot, Jerome went back inside to check on Cynthia's progress. She had been unable to reach her husband. The cell system had joined the other utilities and ceased functioning. He watched the elegant older woman as she moved around the room gathering things, mostly pictures of her students. He remembered when he first met her. When she opened the dance studio, he doubted she would be there long, let alone succeed. However, the energetic, charismatic woman quickly won over the people and soon had full classes.

She always said 'Hi,' to him whenever they passed and often engaged him in conversation. Never one for small talk, Jerome soon found himself drawn into her ever-expanding orbit. She was about the sweetest, nicest person he had ever met, and had great respect for what she was trying to do for the community. He often stopped by to watch or answer her call if she needed something moved or fixed. He found he enjoyed the distraction from an otherwise secluded life.

"I brought you this," he said, picking up the bottle of wine he set down before his violent attack on the intruders.

"Why, Jerome, thank you." Her smile beamed. Too short to reach him, she latched on to his shirt, pulled him down, and gave him a peck on the cheek. "How nice of you to think about me."

"Yeah, well, it's kind of a bribe. I'm giving you this if you promise never to return here."

Her smile faded and he felt bad about ruining the moment.

She glanced around the room. "I already decided that was for the best. No one is ever going to come back—ever, are they?"

Jerome frowned. 'I don't know, Cynthia. One day but that will be a long way off. For now, it's best you're with your family."

She sobbed and placed a gentle hand over her mouth as her eyes clouded with tears. "We haven't been able to reach any of our children. I'm so afraid for them."

He stepped forward and held her. "Then it's time for you to go find out." They stayed that way for a moment before he said, "Come on. It's time to go before it gets too late to be outside."

They exited the studio and Cynthia turned, blew a kiss into the room then closed the door. Jerome had already rolled the bike out and retrieved his spare helmet. Though he seldom wore one himself, he did now to prevent Cynthia from refusing hers. It was a little large for her and wiggled a bit when she shook her head.

He started the bike and she climbed skillfully on behind him. Almost two hours later, they arrived at a cabin in the woods where Kenneth had moved them, citing growing safety concerns. As the two hugged, Jerome gave a wave and drove off, wishing them peace and safety but knowing neither was likely.

It was full dark by the time he arrived back at the apartment building. He didn't like being out at night. The worst predators slid from their hiding places in the dark.

Though he didn't fear a confrontation, he knew the unknown could bring even the bravest down. He also feared the sound of his bike would draw them like zombies after fresh meat.

Twice he avoided people reaching out to grab him as they materialized from the dark like a spirit. Once, he slowed as he heard a woman cry out for help. She sat at the side of the street with a bundle she rocked like a baby. He almost fell for it until he heard a quick footstep scrape on the concrete street to his opposite side. He rode off before the trap could be closed. People were desperate, but rather than put the effort out to find what they needed, they'd rather take someone else's things. Although he had to admit, that wasn't much different now than it was before the pandemic.

Jerome thought about stopping short of the apartment building and walking his bike to avoid making noise, however, that idea quickly vanished when he spotted groups prowling the streets.

At the apartment complex, he hurried to unlock the door and roll the bike inside, though he wasn't fast enough in closing the door. A hand extended out of the darkness and caught the door, yanking it from Jerome's hand.

Jerome scooted to the front of the bike and pulled it with him as he backed toward the elevator. It was awkward work keeping the heavy bike erect from that position, but he needed it as a barrier between him and whoever entered. He had no time to stow the bike away. So as the group of invaders entered and stood studying him, he set the kickstand and prepared for battle.

Six men stood opposite him. Their leader, a stocky Latino, smiled broadly. "Nice bike. I always wanted one like that."

Jerome doubted he even rode a bike, let alone knew the brand of his.

"I think I'd like to have yours. What do you think? You gonna give me your bike?"

Jerome knew whatever he did, it would not matter. They were not here for the bike but to cause damage. Big mistake. He had his finger through the loop of his Ka-bar Pocket Strike ready to pull and had released one of the throwing knives up his sleeve into the other palm. He needed to lessen the odds fast if this confrontation got physical.

Two of the gang climbed the stairs, helping to that effect. One stood back in a relaxed position, taking on more of the role of an interested observer. Three to one were odds he could manage. He focused on the leader. Often if you took down the alpha, the others faltered, unable to adapt to the changing situation. In most cases, minus their leader's bravado, they ran.

"I didn't hear your answer. Are you giving me your bike, or do I have to take it from you?"

Jerome plotted his moves. He had a dozen blades on him. They all had a purpose.

"You're not man enough to ride the bike or take it from me."

From the expression on his face, the answer took the man by surprise. He wasn't used to being told no. He glanced over each shoulder, exchanging knowing smiles with his buddies. "Did you hear that? He says I'm not man enough."

Then his dark eyes narrowed and he focused on Jerome. With an exaggerated flourish, he flicked a knife open. Jerome glanced at it. It was a good pocketknife. The blade locked, which made it an actual threat if the man knew how to use it. "What about now? You still think I'm not man enough to kill you?"

Jerome snorted a derisive laugh. "Just cause you have a knife doesn't make you more of a man. In fact, it tells me you don't feel you're man enough to take me hand-to-hand. You think, no, probably hope the mere sight of that knife will make me cower and beg for mercy. No, I stand by my first observation. You're a coward."

Jerome knew the words would incite the man enough to charge. He roared and ran at Jerome with the knife held to the side, ready to perform a sweeping swipe designed to eviscerate. As the man rushed up one side of the bike, Jerome stepped to the other. Reacting to their leader's actions, the next two men came behind him, while the fourth man looked less relaxed and ready to assist.

In a smooth motion, Jerome lifted his hand and sent the throwing knife on its way. The blade struck the chest of the man to the leader's left, sinking deep. He stood erect, stopped in his tracks, stunned. A curious look appeared on his suddenly less confident face.

As the Latino man came close, Jerome blocked the wide-armed swing, trapping the arm against his body and slashed with the curved blade of the Pocket Strike, severing the carotid and sending a gout of blood spraying against the elevator doors. The man fell, clutching at his neck, the knife long forgotten and clattering to the floor.

After throwing the first knife, Jerome's empty hand found and pulled the Ka-Bar Ontario MKIII from the rigid plastic sheath on his belt. As the second man fell, he was already in motion. He thrust the blade into the third man's side and used it to hold him upright, allowing the Pocket Strike to slice his throat as well.

Stunned by the sudden turn, the fourth man shouted, "Hey! Hey! We need help down here." His panicked voice had been high-pitched and the fright constricted his throat. He turned and banged through the outer door.

Above, Jerome could hear running footsteps. He toyed with the idea of taking them down with throwing knives but decided to give them a chance to live should they be smart enough to take it. As the two men raced down the stairs, they took in the carnage and both made up their minds to live. They ran straight for the door. He could hear one of them retching before the door closed.

Jerome let them go. He didn't enjoy killing. He just never backed down from it when necessary. This would be a lesson to them. Doubtful, but he could hope. The more likely outcome was they'd regroup and come back for him. Maybe it was time for him to pack up and leave, too.

Chapter Four

    Jerome didn't think they'd be back tonight which gave him time. He needed to pack. Unfortunately, riding a bike, even one with saddlebags did not offer room to haul all the items he wanted to take with him, which included food, water, and weapons. He had hard choices to make.
    After putting the bike in the elevator, he went up to his apartment and began organizing. He took out an old, well-used backpack and began to load up. He started with two changes of clothes, then added lightweight packs of food. On top of that, he placed equipment he felt necessary for survival on the road. For the moment, he had no idea where he was going but thought it best and safer to be out of the city where he had a better chance of seeing trouble coming.
    Not wanting to be seen on the ground level, Jerome pried open the elevator doors on the second floor and used the maintenance ladder to climb to the top of the car. There he popped open the escape hatch and lowered himself to the floor. Over several trips, he filled his bags with canned food and bottled water as well as ammo and other needed items. His storage quickly filled with more to go.
    On his third trip back to his apartment, he heard noise from the first floor followed by a host of excited voices and knew he had misjudged the gang's desire for immediate payback. He hurried to his room and bolted all doors. He didn't think they knew which room was his, so he tried to buy time by moving with care.

He repositioned the furniture for defensive use and then organized his arsenal. He had five handguns from a twenty-two caliber up to a forty-five. He set a nine-millimeter on the kitchen counter and a forty caliber on the sofa seat. Then clipped a holster on one hip, slid into a shoulder rig for a second, and finally slipped the forty-five behind his back. After taking two steps, he took the forty-five out, set it on the sofa, placed the forty on the kitchen counter, and slipped the nine-millimeter into his belt. He held the sawed-off shotgun. Last, he slipped the body armor he'd taken off a deceased policeman over his head and secured it in place. He was ready should anyone come knocking.

Jerome squatted behind the sofa and listened for movement in the hallway. It didn't take long. By the sound of the voices, the gang had grown to what he estimated to be about eight. Not insurmountable, but nothing to take lightly. He guessed they were by the stairs. He crept closer to the door and pressed an ear to it. The voice of the person in command was loud enough to understand he was splitting his group into thirds, each taking a floor. That meant he had time. He relaxed, knowing they'd come soon.

While he waited, he thought first about escape options. He could go out the window but preferred not to. He had no cover if anyone happened to see him and was sure this group would be armed. Also, he did not want to give up his equipment and supplies.

Jerome settled in for a siege, though he wondered if it might not be better to engage them while they were searching and knock a few enemy combatants off. The thought had appeal. When they arrived at his door, they'd know where he was and call the entire group. Sure, they'd have to work to get the door down, but he'd have to face them all at once.

He moved to his door. The sound of a door being crashed in was close. They were only two apartments away. With care, he unlocked his deadbolts, then turned the knob for a peek. The door opened inward from left to right, giving him a clear view down the hall to the right. A man walked out of the apartment across the hall and two down from his. He yelled into the apartment one down from Jerome. "This one's clear. Like the others, it looks like someone's already been through it."

A second man came into view. "Yeah, this one's the same."

Two targets were right in view, unprepared for their deaths. Jerome eased the door open with his foot, leveled the shotgun, and fired a barrel at each man. They went down fast, blood splattering the walls.

Jerome quickly cracked the gun and inserted two more cartridges. He stepped into the hall as he snapped the barrel shut. An arm extended from the next apartment with a semi-automatic handgun attached. It fired from less than twenty feet away.

Surprised and angry at his lax technique, he swung the shotgun toward the shooter as he adjusted his height to throw off the shots. The first two shots missed, an amateur shooter. A third round slammed into his vest as he triggered both barrels. The bullet hit with enough force to knock him into the wall and leave him too stunned to reload or move.

Jerome could still see though the pain made his vision blurry. The wall next to the door was pockmarked. He was sure some of the tiny rounds made it through the door. His clouded brain thought it was a good sign that no further shots came his way.

Above him, on the third floor, he could hear the reverberations of running footfalls. They would be coming, and he was defenseless. He had to force his body through the agony spreading across his chest like a full-blown heart attack and get to the safety of his apartment.

He reached for the floor and clawed his way toward the door. Jerome was fortunate that he had only gone two steps from his threshold before the exchange. The footsteps were racing down the stairs. He used his legs to help propel him and was inside the apartment when he heard, "There they are. The killer went inside that apartment."

Jerome bodied the door closed, then reached up and set the lower deadbolt. Someone slammed into the door, shaking it in its frame. He rolled to the side onto his knees. Staying away from the door, he reached back and set the second lock as two bodies slammed into the door.

His breathing came easier as he accepted and adjusted to the pain. He forced himself to his feet as the pounding ceased. Jerome knew what came next. He managed to set the third lock just before the shooting began. He kept away from the door and the path of the flying bullets and crawled to the sofa. It wouldn't offer much protection but did give him some cover. He crawled to the end of the couch and lay down with a view of the door.

With the shotgun reloaded, he waited for the inevitable. It came sooner than expected. Under another furious assault by bodies and bullets, the door gave way and cracked down the middle. He waited a pause to be sure both men were in the same line of sight, then pulled both triggers. The gun rocked in his hands as the 00 buck shredded the two men's faces, arms, and chests, driving both into the hallway.

"You son of a bitch," someone yelled. "You're gonna die." An arm snaked around the door frame and fired blindly into the room. None of the shots were close.

Jerome reloaded the shotgun, then set it down, changing it for the forty-five. He lined up a shot twelve inches to the right of the door frame and fired four rounds, each spaced about a foot apart. The forty-five had more than enough power to penetrate the wall. His second shot found a target, judging by the cry of pain and the heavy thud.

Over the next five minutes, different guns poked through the door from both sides, taking wild shots. Each one fired two or three times before running away to stay out of his range. While he waited for them to rush him, he reloaded the forty-five. He thought he had two shooters on each side. Were there others, or was four all he had to contend with?

The wait dragged on with no further shots fired. He doubted they had moved on and wasn't about to leave his cover to check.

Behind him, his window shattered. He spun fast, looking for invaders. What he saw instead was fire. The bastards had sent a Molotov cocktail into his apartment with the idea of smoking him out.

Chapter Five

Weatherman searched for recognizable landmarks, but he hadn't been to Chicago in a long time. In fact, since the last time he was with the man they were searching for now. With night falling, there was debate as to whether to continue the hunt or find a place to spend the night.

"It's getting harder to see what we're passing," Money said.

"I'm aware," said Weatherman.

"Are you sure we're even in the right area?" asked Blood Rose.

Weatherman sighed. In truth, he wasn't sure of anything. "No."

Rose placed a hand on his shoulder from the back seat of the minivan they were driving. "CC, maybe it's time to quit for the night."

"Yeah. You're right. Start looking for someplace we can defend if necessary."

"Wait!" Money said. "What's that—there." He pointed.

All eyes swung to the left. The shadow of a large building loomed up next to them.

"I think that's it," Weatherman said.

"Yes," said Money. "There's the sign. Guaranteed Rate Field. Home of the Chicago White Sox. Can you find your way from here?"

"I think so, but as I said, it's been a long time."

They were driving north on South Wentworth Avenue. When they reached the intersection of West 35th Street, he pulled into the middle and checked both directions. "I'm sure it's an apartment building east of the stadium."

"That might cover a lot of ground," Rose said. "Any idea the number of apartment buildings there are east of the stadium?"

Weatherman laughed. "I'm sure there's a lot. His building is not large. It's only three or four stories tall and stands off by itself. I know it's not more than a mile from the stadium. When I was here, Slicer took me to a Bears game and we walked to the stadium."

"You realize that as trained and conditioned special forces operatives, that might mean a five-mile trek without breaking a sweat," Money said.

Weatherman laughed again. "True, but I don't think it was that far. Let's do a quick check over a short distance, and if we don't find the building, we stop for the night."

He turned right and traveled down West 35th Street, passing over the I-90 expressway. On the eastern side they slowed and scanned the area. They kept moving without Weatherman spotting the right building. He was sure he'd recognize the building when he saw it. The trouble was seeing in the dark was too difficult.

They drove for five minutes before he turned left on South Michigan Street. This was not the right area. Too many large buildings lined the street. Slicer's apartment building stood off by itself. He went two blocks through sorority and fraternity row, then turned left at East 33rd Street across the campus for the Illinois Institute of Technology. As they returned to the I-90 expressway, he made another left at South La Salle Street, driving the wrong way on the one-way street marking off a search grid.

When they reached West 35th Street again, he stopped. "Okay. I accept defeat. We are in the right area, just not the right place. I doubt we'll find it in the dark. At least not without a sign."

He turned left onto West 35th Street.

Money laughed. "You mean like a man standing on a corner holding a sign reading *This way to the great Slicer.*"

"Yeah, well, he's black, so it might appear as if the sign is floating."

Rose and Money cracked up.

"Maybe he'll send up a flare," Rose said.

"Or use a bullhorn to announce we're getting warmer," said Money.

"Oh, you two are so funny. Instead of cracking wise, why don't you find us a place to spend the night."

"Or maybe send up a flame into the night sky," Rose said, but her tone had changed from snarky to serious.

"What?" said Money picking up on the change of voice.

"You still joking?" asked Weatherman.

"Actually, I'm not. I see a fire. From the level of the flame, I'd say a building was on fire, and it started like on the third floor."

Weatherman braked and they all glanced back and to the right. A fire was growing and appeared to be spreading.

"What are the odds it's your friend?" asked Money.

"I'd say good."

"Can we take a chance that it's not him and just a street gang getting their kicks?" Rose asked.

"Let's at least check it out to be sure." He looked at each, getting nods. As he made the turn, they readied their weapons.

They drove down Dearborn Street passing a park before reaching a T-intersection. Weatherman went right until Federal Street and turned left. The street turned to sod and got rough. Ahead to their left, they could see the fire along the rear of the building.

"I think that's Slicer's building," Weatherman said.

"Of course, it is," Money said.

"We'll leave the van here and approach on foot." Weatherman said. Once out of the car, he took off at a jog, his eyes sweeping the firelit grounds for potential threats. A series of trees behind the building offered them cover. They regrouped inside the trees and found it was a small park-like setting with seating they assumed was for the tenants of the apartment complex.

Money pointed. "There. Two men. Armed. They're looking up at the second-floor window with the fire."

"Damn!" Weatherman said. "I'm almost positive that's Slicer's apartment.

"Do we scare them off or put them down?" asked Rose.

Before she got a response, gunshots were fired. They ducked. The two men fired three rounds each at the window. Weatherman assumed it was to keep the occupant inside. "We put them down." He moved into engagement position, weapon up, knees slightly bent, steps even and unrushed. With one hand he signaled Money to go right, then sent Rose left. They advanced like the elite force they had been trained to be.

Rose found cover behind parked vehicles. Because of his dark skin and clothes, Weatherman was invisible to the shooters. Money was to the far side of the two and not easy to see. Weatherman fired as he moved, stitching a three-shot burst through the closest shooter. The second man didn't have a chance to turn fully around before Rose put him down with her short burst.

As they converged on the bodies, Weatherman gave further directions. "You two enter the building and see what's what. I'll try to get Slicer's attention from here."

Money and Rose moved off toward the entrance. Inside shots could be heard over the growing roar of the fire. Weatherman called to Slicer, but if he was still alive, he could not hear. "Slicer," he shouted twice more, then the firing inside intensified. It was time to assist his team. He hurried to the entrance, did a quick pop check, then advanced inside. He took the stairs as more shots were exchanged. By the time he reached the second floor, the battle was over. A half dozen enemy combatants were down. Rose and Money stood to the side of the open doorway where smoke was billowing out.

Weatherman moved to the door. He was aware of the holes in the wall where someone had shot through. "Slicer," he called. You in there? Slicer."

A cough was followed by, "How do you know that name?"

"Cause we served together, Brother. It's Weatherman."

More coughing, "Weather, is that really you?"

"In the flesh."

A shot was fired through the door.

"Slicer. What the hell you doing man?"

"Just making sure. If you were dumb enough to be standing there, then you weren't the Weatherman I know."

"You satisfied? You done shooting?"

"Yeah. Any more actives?"

"No."

"Then get in here and help me put out this fire."

"Maybe you should come out here."

"Nope. Got too much stuff to save. Hurry before it all burns up."

Weatherman looked at the others, unsure of his next move. When he started forward, Rose said, "You sure about this?"

"Yeah, my friend," Money said. "It wouldn't be the first time an ex-vet went a little bonkers."

"I'll be fine." He tossed the keys to Money. "Bring up the van. Rose, check the perimeter."

As they went to perform their tasks, Weatherman took a deep breath and walked into the smoke-filled apartment.

Chapter Six

With the fire out but still smoking and the windows open to allow airflow, the two men gathered Slicer's belongings. They bagged much of the food items and dropped them out the window to Money. Once that was done, Slicer stepped back and surveyed the space. "It was the first place I could call my own since leaving the military. I wandered for a while, searching for a place that was right for me. Spent my fair share of nights on the streets. Met some interesting people, including a woman who kept telling me how dumb I was for living on the streets when I was obviously much better than the rest of them.

"She told me if she had my potential, she'd never live on the street. It got me to thinking that maybe I could help her and some of the others by getting a place big enough for them to at least have shelter. I told this woman my idea and she smiled and said, 'Oh baby, that's such a great idea but save yourself. The rest of us are beyond saving. We gave up a long time ago. We just been doing it too long. But you, you can be something better. Don't wait too long or you'll become a street zombie like me.'

"Later that night, she OD'd. I carried her to the hospital, but her final breath came long before I arrived. That was my wake-up call. Got a job at a garage service station working on cars. Saved a little money, got myself this place, oh, and one more thing." He smiled. "Let me show you this."

They walked downstairs and Weatherman helped Jerome pull back the elevator doors.

"Now, that's sweet," Weatherman said.

"Yep. My first big purchase since becoming a civilian. Had it two years now." He rolled it out of the car and set it in the hall. As Weatherman admired the ride, Jerome said, "Don't get me wrong, it's great to see you, but why are you here?"

Weatherman frowned and Jerome knew what was coming next was not good.

"I've joined with other special forces operatives, some you know. We made a discovery about this pandemic that has us all nervous and, in all honesty, on the run."

Jerome folded his arms and leaned back against the wall. "Am I gonna want to hear this?"

"No. You decide. Let me ask this though. You got any backup power to that Ham upstairs?"

"No. Never thought I'd need it and I just don't use it that often."

"Been in contact with anyone in the last week?"

"Yeah. A few. Most from the neighborhood."

"What about anyone from the old gang?"

"You mean operators? Yeah. One. Voodoo."

"Marshall? I attempted to reach him but came up empty. You talk to him?"

"Yeah."

"You think he's still alive?"

"Was last week, but when the electricity went . . ." He shrugged.

"He still in New Orleans?"

Jerome nodded. "You gathering folks for a purpose?"

"Not sure. It goes back to whether you want to know or not."

"Man, please don't tell me this is all some big government conspiracy."

Weatherman didn't respond. Instead, he glanced down at the floor.

"Aw, man! Are you kidding me?" He walked away and around the corner out of Weatherman's view. Seconds later, he came back. "Okay, guess I'd better know."

"It is looking like a government conspiracy. It seems some government officials, including military leaders, thought it was time to make a change in how the control was ruled. They have set up five safe zone states and locked them down. You either join or get eliminated."

"Which means; they have some sort of vaccination against the virus."

"Yes. In fact, all military personnel were given the vaccine as part of our normal inoculations before we shipped out. That's why none of us have been infected. When we discovered what was going on, I broke Blood Rose out of a military base in Georgia where she was being held and trained as part of their new militia. Ever since then, we've been on the run."

"So, what you're saying is they were willing to sacrifice millions of lives just to take over the country?"

"Looks that way. There may be way more to what's going on, but that's what we've gathered so far."

"Wait a minute. Back the truck up. Our government-issued inoculations protect us from this virus? But that was almost five or six years ago, just before the last time we shipped out for a duration."

Weatherman nodded. Jerome realized the big man was letting him work it out for himself.

"That can't be. If what you're saying is true, whoever is responsible has been planning it for at least that long."

"At least."

"Aw, man." He turned and walked away again as the implications and the vastness of the conspiracy played out through his mind. Was this all true? Did the government he had served with such pride and tenacity just commit a domestic terrorist attack? Could he walk away knowing what he did now?"

He looked back at Weatherman. He had obviously made his decision.

One of his rescuers came in. He nodded at Jerome and offered his hand. "Money. I've heard great things."

Jerome took it and nodded without speaking.

To Weatherman, Money said, "What's the plan?"

"We should relocate. We don't want to draw any more aggressors."

Money said, "You in?"

"Unsure."

Money accepted the answer. "Vans ready to roll. I'm going to check on Rose." He walked outside.

"We've got a core of good people. I'm gathering more. Like to have you with us but understand if you choose otherwise. Know this. Eventually, a new regime will come around looking for recruits. As a tier two you'll be high on their priority list."

"And?"

Weatherman smiled. "And nothing. You can turn me down but not them. From what I've seen, there's three ways it goes. You accept. You don't, and they take you anyway, or you don't, and they eliminate you as a potential threat."

Jerome frowned at him in disbelief.

"I would not lie to you, Brother. Whatever you decide, it's up to you. Make up your own mind. We're south if you want to join us. I need paper and pencil."

Jerome led him up to his apartment and dug out the notepad and pen from a kitchen drawer. Weatherman jotted down general directions and handed the pad to Jerome. "I can't say for sure how long we're going to be there. I'm not even sure where we're going next. It's time for us to go. Let's find a place to bed down and you can make your decision in the morning."

"That I can do."

"You know the neighborhood, so you take point."

"Some things never change. Send the black man to the front. Do you see a red shirt on me?"

Weatherman chuckled at the reference. "I have no sympathy." He leaned closer and whispered. "Don't tell anyone, but I'm black too."

Jerome gasped and placed a hand over his mouth. He rolled the bike outside and waited for Weatherman to mount up. He led down Federal Street to a place called Legends Farm. They turned in and parked in front of a long narrow building. As they got out, they surveyed the grounds. It was an open field to the north. Behind the building to the south were greenhouses.

Jerome said, "I know the person who runs the place. It's best she sees me first."

He walked to the building and rapped lightly on the door. "Sister, it's me, Jerome."

"Jerome? Why are you here so late?" She sounded nervous. He didn't blame her.

"Someone tried to burn down my apartment building. I need a place to stay the night."

"I don't know, Jerome."

"I understand. I'll go."

"Where? Where will you go?"

"Sister, don't worry about it. I'll be fine. You should also know I have three friends with me. So, I understand your hesitation. We'll move on and find someplace else to spend the night."

"You vouch for these friends?"

"Yes, Sister, I do."

"And it's only for the night?"

"It is."

Silence.

"Step back away from the door."

Jerome did, giving her the necessary space she needed to feel safe about whatever she was doing.

The door opened and a small round black woman reached a hand out and dropped something on the ground. She shut the door fast and hard. Jerome picked the item up and found it to be a key ring with three keys on it.

The voice spoke through the closed door. "Those keys will get you into the other building. Please Jerome, don't destroy my trust."

"I won't. Thank you, Sister." He turned and rejoined the group. "Sister Rachel has agreed to let us stay the night in that building." He pointed to an identical narrow structure a short distance away. They drove down and entered the building. It was stuffy as if closed for a while. It was a converted mobile home with a room at each end and an open space in the middle. There was no kitchen though there was a bathroom.

"Grab some space," Jerome said.

Rose embraced Jerome. "It's good to see you again."

"And you as well."

She moved past and called over her shoulder, "I've got the back room down here."

Money motioned with his head. "I'll take this one. Do we need to set a watch?"

Weatherman looked at Jerome.

"Nah. I think we're good here."

Weatherman said, "What have we got here?" He dropped his tall frame into a well-worn upholstered chair.

"This is a working community farm. It's all organic and self-sustaining, with its own water supply and septic powered by a series of small windmills. The water will run, and the toilet does work. Sister Rachel is the only one left here. They utilized volunteers for the most part and tried to benefit the community. I come here a couple times a week. The food will rot and go to waste, so she lets me take what I need of the vegetables they grow here."

"Maybe she'll let us take food in the morning. Fresh produce may get difficult to find with no one to work the fields."

"I can ask."

Chapter Seven

They woke early the next morning with the sun barely peeking above the horizon. Sister Rachel was already in the fields, weeding a line of broccoli. Jerome walked to her with Rose behind. Sister Rachel stretched and placed her hands on her lower back. The sight of Jerome approaching brought a smile to her sweat-coated face. The sight of Rose with the AR made her flinch.

Jerome raised a hand. "It's alright, Sister. She's a friend. You know in these troubled times many people carry weapons to protect themselves. She is no threat."

Though she didn't flee, it was obvious she was not thrilled to be so close to an armed person.

Jerome stopped eight feet short of the small round woman. "How have you been, Sister? Is there anything you need?"

"I can always use help with the crops. You know that. Not one staff or volunteer has shown up in four days now. I can't let this all go to waste. People depend on this food."

Rose slung the rifle behind her. "What do you need done?"

Sister Rachel's jaw went slack, then worked up and down a couple of times before she said, "Ah, well, if you don't mind, that next plot over there needs to be weeded."

Rose spied a bucket with hand tools and gloves and picked it up. She donned the gloves, knelt, and went to work. Her actions eased Sister Rachel's tension.

"Did someone really burn down your apartment building, Jerome?"

"They tried, Sister. My friends arrived in time to rescue me, or I might be barbequed Jerome this morning." She glanced nervously past Jerome's shoulder. He assumed she spotted Money and Weatherman.

"Do you expect more trouble?"

"These are current times, Sister. Trouble will always be right around the corner. I'm not sure if I'll be staying in the neighborhood. You should think about leaving, finding someplace safe. With other people."

"You think it's going to get that bad?"

"They attacked me and I'm more of a threat than you are. Someone will come eventually. I'd feel better knowing you were someplace safe. Are you spending all your nights here?"

"Yes. I don't have transportation, and as I said, no one has come for days. I don't feel comfortable walking that far to get home."

"Then let me take you home."

She chewed on her lower lip as she thought about his words. "No. No, I can't leave now. At least not until the crops come in. People will need a food supply more now than ever. I can't abandon them. Besides, I'd have no way to get back. I can't rely on you to drive me from place to place. No. This is where I belong."

"Sister. The people who see the value here will not hesitate to take it all for themselves."

"Me and the food are in God's hands, Jerome. He will see to my well-being and that the food gets to those who need it most."

Weatherman joined them. His large frame caused her to take a step back and have to bend to look at his face.

"Hi, ah, Sister Rachel. My name is Darwin. You have an amazing place here. It's great what you have accomplished."

Though startled by his sudden approach, Sister Rachel recovered and said, "Thank you, Darwin. We have worked hard to get where we are."

"How long have you been here?"

"Oh, just over two years. It took a while to establish and has grown to over two acres now."

"Wow! That's amazing. Do you serve a specific community, or is this for everyone?"

"We grow culturally relevant food with and for the local community through sustainable agricultural practices. It's all organic and one hundred percent is either sold, donated, or composted." She beamed with pride. "We envision a world in which every person can access their right to foods that can benefit their health, community, and environment."

She sounded like an advertisement. Jerome smiled at the well-rehearsed slogans and mission statements. "Sister, would it be possible to take some of the produce from the greenhouse?"

"For your own use?"

"Yes, Sister. It will be just for the four of us."

"Ah, if I may, we have three others with us at another location. If it's alright, I'd like to take them fresh produce, too. You can check what we take to make sure it isn't too much."

"Of course. That's what we're here for."

"That's what you're here for," Jerome said.

She gave him a blank look.

"There is no we anymore. It's just you." He turned to Weatherman. "I've been trying to convince her that it isn't safe to be here alone."

Weatherman said, "Slicer's right, Sister—"

"Slicer?"

"Ah," he glanced at Jerome.

He cringed.

Jerome never wanted Sister Rachel to know that side of him. It had been a call sign he hadn't heard or gone by since leaving the service.

"It's just a nickname," Weatherman said, trying to cover his mistake. "I mean Jerome. Jerome is right. This is no place to be at night."

"Thank you for your concern, Darwin, but I have decided to stay until the crops have been harvested. Please, you and your friends help yourself to whatever is left in the greenhouse. I fear it will go to waste otherwise."

"Thank you, Sister." Weatherman turned and walked away.

Jerome bent to pick up a bucket. They had all been prepped for the volunteers to use when they came. Each one had hand tools and gloves for weeding. He walked to a section to the right of where Rose toiled and began weeding.

They worked for more than an hour before Rachel said, "I'm beat. Why don't we take a break to eat?"

"Sounds good to me," Jerome said.

Behind the first building, she said, "You all wait here and I'll pick us some breakfast."

Weatherman and Money had already picked a bucket of assorted veggies, including tomatoes, cucumbers, zucchini, and green beans.

She came back with an assortment of her own. "Jerome, would you light the grill please?" She went inside, returning minutes later with a cutting board, a stack of paper plates, a chef's knife, a decanter of olive oil, and containers of sea salt, rosemary, oregano, and basil. She sliced the veggies, tossed them in oil then set them on the hot grill. As they cooked, she seasoned them. Minutes later, they were all eating the variety. Jerome had to smile. Sister Rachel was a natural for this type of work. If it had been any other time, he was sure the volunteer recruitment speech would begin.

When the meal was over, the others offered thanks and said their goodbyes, and went to the van. Jerome stayed behind. "Sister, please consider what I have told you. I'll be around for another day or so. I'll come back and check on you, and you can let me know your decision."

"I can tell you now, Jerome. I'll be staying."

He was sure she would. "I'll stop by anyway."

She hugged him. It was the first time he could recall ever having physical contact with her. It was her way of saying goodbye.

He joined the others at the street.

"That's a good person," Weatherman said.

"Yes, she is. I don't want anything to happen to her."

"You staying then?"

He looked back at the building as if able to see through it to where he had left her. "For a while. I've got others to check on before I make any long-term decisions."

"Understood, Brother," Weatherman said. "You know where we'll be, though I'm not sure for how long."

They clasped hands through the sliding door, then Weatherman scooted back inside, closed the door and the minivan drove off.

Chapter Eight

With reluctance, Jerome climbed on his Indian Motorcycle and brought it to life with a roar. He rode away with a plan for his day. He had three close friends he wanted to check on and an assortment of others to look in on. Some he knew for sure were still alive. Others, he wasn't sure. If he was leaving the city, he wanted to make sure those he was close to were taken care of and safe.

As he rode, he ran what Money and Weatherman had told him about the massive government conspiracy. If it was true, hell, if any part of it was true, mass murder had been committed. He knew there was little he could do to reverse the course of an organization that well established and ruthless, but he wasn't sure he could not get involved. Hadn't he stood against injustice both in the military and in his neighborhood? This was injustice on a grand scale. Still, he hadn't made up his mind yet. Overall, however long that might be, it might be healthier to stay as far away from Weatherman and his people as possible.

He rolled on, lost in thought. What difference could such a small band of people make despite their valor and integrity? They were outmatched in every possible important statistic from personnel to armament to logistics. It didn't matter that their cause was righteous. What would any of it matter without the ability to communicate to the masses? Building one person at a time, regardless of their pedigree, was too little too late. Yet his brother in arms had come to him knowing the type of man he was.

A new thought entered his mind. The minivan had driven away with a lot of his food and extra weapons. He sighed. Was that incentive enough to join the rebel forces?

He pushed the problem from his mind for a moment and focused on those he was about to see. Two of the three most important to him were former military. Though both were grunts, they had established themselves as top-notch warriors both in training and combat. The third was a current Chief Petty Officer in the Coast Guard who was having issues with being passed over for a promotion.

One of the two men had been a street punk who had turned his life around. He had great respect for Alonzo Moore. The man had been through a lot, much of it violent and bloody, but he'd risen from the streets to own several small, black-owned businesses that had prospered and grown into a brand.

His first stop was to see Master Sergeant Michael Bedford. Sarge was a twenty-one-year vet who had taken shrapnel in his leg and now walked with a limp and the use of a cane. Though he still walked ramrod straight, his pace had been slowed by the injury. That was not going to stop Sarge. His fierce pride did not allow him to appear as anything less than his best.

Sarge lived in a four-story apartment building closer to the downtown area. The building was rundown and the neighborhood transient. Jerome suspected it was all his pension allowed him to afford. Though he never complained, he was sure the man had the same thoughts he had himself: 'After all I've been through for this country, is this all there is?'

Jerome pulled up on the sidewalk in front of the old red brick building and glanced around. He had passed more than twenty bodies left to rot on the streets. Rodents had already begun feasting. Soon diseases of other kinds would rise, perhaps killing off the rest of humanity. Yes, perhaps it was time to get out of the city, even if it weren't to join Weatherman.

He rolled the bike to the door. Unless he took the center pole out, the double doors weren't wide enough to permit entry with the bike. He scanned the area. No one was about. Was it safe to chance it, especially considering what he had in the saddlebags? He was reluctant but had no alternatives. Why did Sarge have to live on the top floor? He'd just have to be fast.

Jerome left the bike as close to the outer wall as possible to keep it from sight, then raced inside and up the stairs. By the time he reached the fourth floor, he was winded and chastised himself for getting to that point in his conditioning.

He paused, not wanting to arrive at Sarge's door sucking air like some recruit. Sarge would ride him forever. He took one controlled breath and then knocked on the door. He pressed his ear to the heavy wood door and could hear the distinct shuffle and tap of Sarge's approach.

"I will tell you two things," the voice called out in his best sergeant's tone. "One, if I don't know you and you are here to perform mischief, go away. Two, if I do or do not know you and you think to get the better of me, run now."

"Sarge, it's me, Jerome."

The tapping came closer. Sarge spoke through the door. "You will stand four feet from the door, dead center to my peephole. You will keep your hands to the side with the palms facing forward. If I see any sudden moves, I will blast you through the door. Did I make myself clear?"

"Understood, Sarge." Jerome gave him his best raw recruit response, loud and defined, then stood exactly as recommended for his safety.

"Why are you here?"

"Sarge, I'm not here for any reason other than to talk."
"So, talk."
"Sarge. Come on."
"You armed?"
"Hell, yeah." Jerome heard a grunt, but whether signifying agreement or unease, he wasn't sure. Sarge knew him and knew the weapons he had secreted around his body. Well, some of them. He may never know the full extent of his personal armament. He only wore the one rig at the moment. The full harness was stowed in the saddlebags. Then, of course, there were the guns.

"If you make a move toward any weapon, you will not live to bring it to bear."

"Understood, Sarge."

Moments later, satisfied he was not a threat and who he said he was, the various locks released, and the door swung inward. Sarge stood to the side of the threshold, his heavy wooden cane was hooked in his pants pocket and a pump-action shotgun was leveled at his torso.

Sarge was a short, sturdy man in his early fifties. His dark penetrating, intelligent eyes held the promise of pain should his directives not be followed to the T. His black skin glistened with a patina of sweat. He looked like he could still serve with honor. They stood still for several seconds as Sarge waited for something. Whatever that was, Jerome was done. "Sarge, what are we doing here?"

"Question is, what are you doing here? You come to rob the old man?"

"What? No. I—"

"Then why are you here?"

Sarge was acting strange, and Jerome wondered whether the old man was losing his mind. Jerome decided to tell him the reason to see if his friend changed his defensive and suspicious stance. "Someone tried to attack me last night. They set my apartment on fire."

"So, what? You thought you'd come here? Maybe think I'll be nice enough to let you in, share all my food stores?"

"Ah, no. I came to let you know I may be leaving the area. The city is no longer safe."

That registered in Sarge's eyes. The gun wavered and lowered an inch. "Leaving?" His voice faltered with disbelief. "Where-where would you go?"

"Unknown. I was presented with an interesting option which is my other reason for being here."

Sarge gave a knowing nod as if he already knew what Jerome was going to say, then stepped back and motioned with the barrel of the shotgun for him to enter. He lowered the gun and Jerome entered. Sarge stepped into the hall and scanned both directions before closing and relocking the door.

He pinned the gun between his arm and torso and followed Jerome into the kitchen. "Get you something to drink?"

"No thanks. My bike is on the street, exposed, and my bags are full. I can't stay long."

"Yep. Been lots of activity lately as people begin to understand the extent of the situation. Lots of people searching for food and water and not caring about what they have to do to get it. Get down to your bike. I'll join you in a minute."

Jerome hurried to the door but waited. He knew Sarge had a certain way of unlocking the door. As soon as the door opened, he hurried out and trotted down the stairs. As he reached the last flight, he could see a rail-thin man hunched over his bike, pulling out his food items.

He launched down the stairs pulling the handgun from the holster at his back. Jerome slammed through the outer door startling the man. He stumbled and fell backward, cans of food spilling from his arms and rolling away.

He saw the gun and backpedaled on his hands and feet. "No. No. No. No. Don't shoot. I'm sorry, man. I was just—so hungry. Please. Just don't kill me." He stopped moving and lifted both hands in front of his face, a flesh and bone shield.

"Stay right where you are. You move, I fire."

"Okay. Okay. Please. Don't kill me." The man shook with fear though Jerome suspected the shakes were enhanced by withdrawals. He gathered the cans and replaced them in the bags as Sarge exited the door. He held the shotgun on the man as Jerome strapped the bags closed.

"Get up," Jerome ordered the man.

"Sure. Sure. I'm sorry. I didn't know it was anyone's bike. I swear."

"Whatever." Jerome extended a can of kidney beans toward the man.

The man stared at it in disbelief and hesitated to take it.

"Go on."

The man's hand shook as he took the can, then withdrew quickly.

"Go now."

"Yes, Sir. Thank you, Sir. God bless you."

The man held the can in his arms like he was cradling a baby. He moved away on an unsteady gait. Jerome doubted the man would survive much longer.

"You're too soft-hearted, Jerome. The weak will be culled and there's nothing you can do to prevent it. It's a natural process. The strong survive."

"Doesn't mean I can't show compassion. Once we lose that, we lose any hope of recovering humanity. If it helps him survive a little longer," he shrugged, "who knows what he might yet become."

"Yeah, a more desperate killer."

He faced his friend. Sarge had always been a hard man. Whether from the life-altering wound he took to his leg and being forced to leave the Marines, a life he cherished, or the current events they now faced, he had changed.

"So, tell me about these plans of yours, or from what it sounds like, lack of plans."

Jerome smiled. "During the attack last night, I was rescued by a small group of fellow vets. When the fight was over, they filled me in on what they've discovered."

"Which is?"

"This," he motioned with an arm toward the streets, "was a deliberate attack by our own government."

Sarge took a step back like he'd been slapped. "Bull shit!"

"Sarge, I know these people. They're tier one and two operatives and not susceptible to conspiracy theories. What they laid out to me sounds entirely plausible. I believe them."

"You do? I'm thinking you swallowed the Kool-Aid. So, you thinking about running off to join the circus? Is that your plan?"

"I haven't decided if I'm joining them or not, but I have decided it's time to leave the city."

"You could just move to another place. Hell, there's plenty of units here."

"No, Sarge. It's getting too dicey around here. Soon it will get to a point where someone will pop you for a bottle of water."

"It was that way before the pandemic."

"Can't deny it, but I'd rather be someplace where I can see trouble coming. That means getting out of the city. Besides, with all the dead bodies on the streets, it won't be long before the rats are the bigger problem." He studied his friend as he soaked in the information. "Sarge, it's not safe here. I'm making the rounds to close friends to let them know I'm leaving, and then I'm gone."

"Do you honestly believe the government is responsible for releasing this virus?"

"I'm not sure what I believe. It's a toss-up between whether I want to get as far away from whatever is happening and learning more." A thought came to him. "You know, you could come with me. We can get out of the city and decide what to do then."

"And where would we go?"

"There's bound to be plenty of vacancies wherever we go."

"You plan on riding me on the back of your motorcycle?"

Jerome hadn't thought about that. "Guess we'll have to find you a vehicle."

"You mean steal one."

Jerome laughed. "In case you haven't noticed, there're not many people around to care. Besides, it's not like there's any law enforcement."

"What if we take a vehicle that belongs to someone alive. We can't take their only means of transportation."

"You have strange reasonings. You know that? I'll tell you what. We'll look for one we're sure the owner will not be coming back to collect."

"You mean, cause they're dead." Sarge looked away, clearly disturbed by his thoughts. He had an old-fashioned sense of right and wrong, and taking someone else's property was wrong. He would have to adjust his thinking.

"Yeah, okay. I could do that."

Jerome wasn't sure what surprised him more. The fact Sarge was willing to take a vehicle that didn't belong to him or that he was willing to move at all.

"You'll have to give me time to get things packed."

"How much do you need?"

"Don't know. Coupla hours."

"That's perfect. I want to see some other people first. I'll swing back when I'm done, and we can find you a vehicle."

He nodded. "Good. Now we have the start of a plan." Without another word, he did an awkward pivot and went inside. Jerome watched him go and wondered what he was going to find upon his return. He'd believe Sarge was going to leave when he saw him in the seat of whatever vehicle he was going to drive away in.

Chapter Nine

As he rode, Jerome thought back to when he first met Sarge. It was at a Kali Eskrima Filipino martial art class. The style, also known as Arnis, took in not only open hand combat but had a strong, weapon-based fighting system, including the use of sticks, knives, and improvised weapons. Although it's a weapons-heavy style, every blade technique translates smoothly to the empty hand. Kali Eskrima places a strong emphasis on angles of attack rather than specific slashes utilizing triangular-based footwork, so the practitioner is always off-center to the opponent.

All hand-to-hand attacks use these angles, allowing avoidance of punches and kicks as well as the bladed hand. One of the core concepts of the Arnis art involves trapping and disarming using the "live hand" or the extra hand without a weapon.

Jerome had become proficient, if not expert, in multiple hand-to-hand combat forms, especially with a knife, including the Russian Spetznaz training program. His particular interest in that training was to learn about the ballistic knife.

The special forces ballistic knife is a badass hybrid blade and projectile. The blade of a ballistic knife can be fired with the push of a button and travels about five meters at around 40mph. Jerome owned one, smuggled back to the states after the most intense knife fight of his life. The Russian sleeper agent had caused him damage, but ironically it was his brief Spetznaz training that allowed him to dodge the fired projectile blade and bury a throwing knife into the man's left eye. The Spetsnaz training also included throwing knives, a skill he was already an expert in, however, the additional knowledge only enhanced his keen abilities. Jerome had tested the compressed air weapon but had never carried it.

Jerome had already mastered the Marine Corps Martial Arts program, which was a brutal hand-to-hand training with a mix of Brazilian jiu-jitsu, boxing, wrestling, and Muay Thai, with a substantial portion of the training in knife fighting techniques.

He remembered the first day of their Arnis training when the then recently retired Sarge had trouble finding an opponent willing to spar with a cripple. The cocky twenty-year-old opponent assigned to him complained to the instructor that it wasn't fair for him to fight an old cripple. With two quick moves, Sarge had the man on his back with the end of the cane pointed dangerously close to his eye. The enraged expression on Sarge's face had everyone in the dojo worried about the fate of the young man.

Sarge broke his anger, stepped back, and snapped to attention. He offered a quick bow, then walked toward the door. Jerome stopped him. "I'll spar with you."

Sarge gave him a once-over glance, then grunted, and continued toward the door. Jerome challenged him. "You won't put me down like you did that kid."

Sarge stopped. "Come on, old man, take me down."

From that moment on, they were partners and eventually friends, and yes, Sarge did take him down, multiple times.

He arrived outside a twenty-four-story building in the heart of the once bustling downtown. The building was co-owned by a one-time street punk and drug dealer, Alonzo Moore. Moore had turned his life around after escaping near death on the streets by enlisting in the army. To his great surprise, he found he liked the routine, the authoritarian lifestyle, and the tight discipline, all of which had been missing from his life until that time.

Moore not only liked his new life, he thrived under the hard and heavy workload. His efforts earned him two quick promotions. Then at the prodding of a sergeant, he volunteered for Ranger Training. The brutal training had him tested to limits he never knew he possessed, but upon graduation, he had a newfound confidence that had him believing his true potential had not yet been reached. He wore the tan beret of the 75th Regiment with pride but strived to go even further. Throughout his four tours, he always pushed to learn and grow both mentally and physically. He took every form of severe training he could find, which was where they first met. Aside from Weatherman, Moore, code name AS for alien species because of his intense desire to be better than human, was the first human he had ever met who matched his own desires and drive.

When Moore got out of service, he turned that same ambition into a business that grew beyond his wildest aspirations. Now he sponsored and encouraged young people who might otherwise end up where he had once been.

Moore was a few years older than Jerome and had been well established in his growing business empire by the time he was home from service. They had met for the first time in five years at a grand opening of a young black man's coffee house that Moore had sponsored, and they had been close ever since.

Jerome wheeled his bike into the grand lobby of the building. The semi-circular, polished marble front desk was unoccupied. Jerome wheeled the bike behind the desk and froze. A man in a suit lay on the floor. He was dead, but the cause was not the usual disease. This death was caused by several gunshot wounds to the body that entered the chest and blew out large holes in the back. The other item of interest was the still pooling blood on the shiny floor. This was a fresh kill. He drew his gun and flicked off the safety. Was this AS, or was someone after him?

He peered around the corner and studied the corridor to the elevators as he focused on any sounds. He saw and heard nothing.

Jerome patted the dead man's pockets and then checked his belt. Attached was a key ring on an extending line. He set the gun on the desktop, pulled his Ka-bar fighting knife, and sliced through the line. He noticed a shoulder holster. The gun was missing.

After another check of the corridor, Jerome moved to the first door down the hall on the right. He had no idea which key unlocked it, so was forced to try them all. The tenth key on the ring of twenty unlocked the door.

From a tour of the building during an early visit, Jerome knew this to be the security guard's lounge. It housed a small kitchenette, lockers, a bathroom, and security monitors. He propped the door open with a chair, then rolled his bike inside and relocked the door. With the key in his pocket, he moved with haste toward the bank of elevators. AS might need help.

He hurried past the elevators to the stairs. At the fire door, he paused, then cracked it open. He listened for a moment before entering. As he peered up the long flight of stairs, he wished his friend had chosen an office on the second floor rather than the top.

Jerome started up, keeping a steady pace and his eyes and gun focused upward. He reached the eleventh floor before he heard a sound that froze him. Above, a door opened. The change in sound was instant. Someone was coming down. From the grunts, groans, and gasps, that someone was injured. Before the door sealed shut, Jerome could hear sporadic gunshots. A battle was going on, and his friend might be in trouble.

He pressed into the wall, trained his gun up, and waited. The man coming down was struggling. He assumed the man had been wounded in the exchange. His progress was too slow for Jerome and possibly for AS. He moved with cautious haste, hoping the man's pained exclamations covered any noise he made. The thirteenth floor was as far as he felt he could go without drawing attention. The injured man was two flights above.

When he reached the fourteenth floor the man cried out and stopped moving. Jerome could hear the man crying. He edged forward to peer up but had no vantage point to see him. Had the man become aware of his presence? He listened. From the man's whispered dialogue to himself, he realized the man was praying and begging God not to let him die.

Jerome climbed the stairs until he spotted the man sitting against the wall of the landing between the two floors. His head was down and his bloody hands covered his stomach. He had been gut-shot and would die soon. Before that happened, he needed information. He approached. At the top step, he scuffed his foot to draw the man's attention. As the head lifted and he spotted Jerome through tear-filled eyes, a bright light of hope lit his face.

He was a small Latino man with a scraggly black beard. "Please. Help me."

The man's gun was in a full belt holster like he was in the old west. Jerome lowered slightly. "I'm here to help. What's going on upstairs?"

"Please. I'm bleeding. Can you make it stop?"

"Yes. Yes. Just lay down here and let me look." As he guided the man to the floor, he slipped the gun out and slid it into his belt behind his back. "Move your hands so I can see." He pretended to examine the wound, trying hard not to get blood on his hands. Not for any fear of disease. He didn't want his hands slick if he needed to fight.

The wound was bad. The blood seeped and there didn't appear to be an exit wound. Since most rounds were powerful enough to go through a body, he had to assume the bullet was either small caliber or had hit something to prevent its passing. "How's it going up there?"

"Can you help me?"

"Yes. That's what I'm trying to do but talk to keep your mind off the wound. Now, what's going on up there?"

"We got the rich guy pinned down in his office. I think it's just him and one of his security people." The man gasped as Jerome lifted his shirt to expose the wound. "Mateo is negotiating for the food supply."

"How many do we have?"

"Six, no seven. We lost three."

"Okay." Jerome leaned back to cover sliding the knife out.

"What are you doing? Help me."

"There's no help for you."

The man's eyes widened as he glimpsed the knife just before Jerome slid it between his ribs and into his heart. He wiped the blade on the man's pants, then hurried up the stairs to the twenty-fourth floor.

Chapter Ten

The gunshots were louder now. They echoed down the hallway and through the fire door. Jerome knew the entire top floor was a combination office and apartment. A receptionist's desk was to the left, directly in front of where the elevators opened. Further to the left was the apartment. To the right was the office.

The body of a woman was slumped back in a chair. She had taken multiple rounds to her chest and most likely died instantly. The battle was to the right. No one was currently in sight, but he heard voices. Jerome called to mind the floor plan of the office. Around the corner were six workstations. Three to the right along the wall of windows and three to the left. Beyond those against the outer wall was a series of three small offices. To the left were the larger rooms: two conference rooms and Moore's and his partner's massive offices. Jerome had never met the partner and wondered if one even existed or was it a creation of Moore's for some unknown reason.

He reached the corner and peered around. The fight was happening down the hall near Moore's office. The office door was riddled with holes, as was the wall to the left of the door. So far, the glass window to the right of the door sported round holes but still stood.

Men were in the doorways of both conference rooms poking guns out. A lull in the battle was in progress, making it difficult for Jerome to advance. He ducked and crawled to the front desk on the left. He now had a clear line of sight down the hall to Moore's office door.

Jerome counted three men against the side walls of the conference rooms, two on the left of the hall, one on the right. He spotted three different guns pointed out the conference room doorways, two on the right and one on the left. If there were others, they were hidden. If the dead man's tally had been accurate, one person was still unaccounted for.

He had to assume that Moore was still alive, otherwise the invaders would be inside his office. Something was off. If these men were here for food, the apartment was the more obvious target. Why were they assaulting the office? Two of them could keep Moore pinned down while the others stripped the apartment unless they couldn't get inside.

One of the men from the doorway fired a round. They talked in conspiratorial whispers across the hallway. One of the men darted from the left side conference room and huddled with the three on the outside. They must have come to the same conclusion. The four men moved toward Jerome. He was out of time and had to act.

From the floor, he moved enough to see past the desk and fired. The front two men dropped. He kept pulling the trigger, wounding a third man. He stopped firing, scooted behind the desk, and reloaded. Bullets whizzed past and slammed into the metal side of the desk. He was thankful that Moore had spared no expense when outfitting the outer workstations. The desk stopped the rounds.

Perhaps realizing that the tide had turned and help had arrived, Moore and a slim Asian woman exited the office with guns blazing. Moore held two 1911s while the woman fired an Uzi. They walked without fear of being shot, hoping they hit their targets with overwhelming force before anyone took a shot at them. Rounds tore through the conference rooms cutting down whoever was inside.

The two remaining men were trapped between Moore and Jerome. The woman cut down the first man with a long burst, making him dance in his final moments. Moore turned to the last man, the one Jerome had wounded. The man begged. "Please. Don't kill me. I don't want to die."

Moore said, "Then you shouldn't have come in here." He fired both guns twice, silencing the pleas.

As the echoes of the last shots died away, Moore called out, "Jerome. That you?"

Jerome noticed the woman was working her way to get an angle on him.

"It is. You need to stop her now before we have a problem."

Moore spoke to her in an Asian dialect and the woman stopped moving. However, she did not lower the weapon.

"AS, if she doesn't lower that gun, we're going to have a problem."

"She's making sure there isn't going to be a problem. How are you here?" His tone was challenging.

"Oh, that how it is? You're welcome, by the way."

"For?"

"Oh, I don't know, just the Marines rescuing the Rangers once again."

"As if that ever happened. I like you, my friend, which is why we're still talking, but you need to convince me that you weren't part of this attack."

Jerome understood his concern. Though it irritated him that Moore didn't trust him better, he knew he had to be convincing to avoid having to kill his friend. If that was even possible.

"I'm only here to say goodbye. I'm leaving the city. I just happened to be here when this was going on. As for me being a part of this, I'm not even justifying that with a response. You should just know me better."

"Troubling times, my friend. Not sure who to trust anymore."

"Understood."

"Tell me more about this leaving plan."

Jerome focused his hearing and heard the scuff of a shoe. "I will, but you need to stop moving for both of our sakes."

"Done. Talk."

"Street punks tried to burn me out of my apartment. I got help from a very surprising source. An old special-ops mate name of Weatherman."

"Weatherman?" The surprise was evident in his tone.

"You know him?"

"No. But I know of him. He's a fucking legend. Go on."

"He was with a couple of other operatives. They told me a story about this pandemic that you won't believe. I came here to relay the tale as I was given it and let you know I'm out of here."

"Huh! The Marines bugging out. Typical. So, what's this story?"

"I'll tell you, but first have your friend there set her weapon down on the desk and back away."

Silence greeted the request.

"I know you've got your guns ready and have moved into position to shoot. I'm trusting that you won't shoot me if I stand."

"Okay. I won't as long as your hands are empty."

"They won't be, but the gun will not be up."

"Alright." He spoke to the woman, who responded in harsh words. She glared at Jerome but did as Moore instructed. She set the Uzi down hard, then backed away two measured steps. Jerome was sure she could get to the weapon fast if necessary.

Jerome lifted one hand above the desk, then got to one knee. He poked his head out from the opposite side of the desk and saw what he expected. Moore had both guns trained on the top of the desk. "Come on, AS, I'm not the threat here."

In slow motion, Moore lowered one gun but held the other unwavering. Jerome sighed. It was going to be step by step. He rose above the desk, keeping his gun aimed downward. If Moore was going to fire, he was defenseless.

When no bullet came for him, Jerome set his gun down on top of the desk and backed away. Only then did Moore lower his second gun.

He gave a slow nod of approval, then said, "So, what's this revelation that Weatherman laid on you?"

Over the next twenty minutes, Jerome relayed what he had been told and answered questions though he had few answers.

"Are you going to join Weatherman?"

"Undecided. Not sure if I want to get involved in a government conspiracy. I may just bug out to parts unknown. Sarge is coming with me."

At the mention of the older man's name, Moore smiled. "He's still alive and kicking, eh?"

"Yep, and as feisty as ever. He was a little untrusting as well. Must be a military thing."

"Or maybe it's just you."

Jerome grunted. "Maybe so. Anyway, I'm out. Just wanted to say goodbye and wish you luck. What are you going to do?"

"Guess stay here and live the good life."

"Yeah. That's you. Well, Brother, stay safe." He offered his hand, which made the woman twitch.

Moore grabbed it in a firm grip. "You as well. I'd be interested to learn more about this plot."

"Sorry. If you want to know more, you'll need to find Weatherman."

"I realize we never served together, only trained, but I don't see you as someone who walks away from a righteous fight."

He nodded toward Moore, gazed at the woman for a moment, then exited. He had one more person to visit before joining Sarge.

Chapter Eleven

He found Meredith Clark on her back, on a worn sofa in an alley with a line of men waiting their turns. He knew right then he should leave her to her fate, but for the sake of an old friendship and for the brief relationship they had once enjoyed, he waded through the eager men, tossing them aside.

Near the front of the line, he met with more resistance and was forced to cut one suitor, sending him running from the alley holding his bleeding arm. As he reached Merri, one man was just climbing off. Jerome latched on to the back of his shirt collar and ripped him away. He fell into the others amidst their vehement protests about '*no cuts* and '*wait your turn.*' He flashed his knife to emphasize the type of cuts he might be dishing out.

As expected, Meredith was barely conscious. Someone in the bunch must have offered her drugs for the pleasure of her body. She was most likely unaware of the abuse her body had taken. She lay naked, with her legs spread wide. Her body was slack as if it didn't have any muscle tone. Her head hung back over the armrest. Her hair was greasy and knotted. She had bite marks on her breasts. Her eyes were closed. He shook her, but she moaned. "That's good, Baby. Oh yeah. That's the spot."

He whirled on the men. "What did she take?" When no one responded, he grabbed the nearest man and shoved the tip of his knife under his chin. The man squealed in terror.

"I don't know honest. I wasn't here first. I don't know what they gave her."

"Somebody does. I'm not punishing anyone. I just need to know who has the supply. I'm willing to pay."

"How much?" a voice called from the back.

"Depends on what it is?"

"Meth and ecstasy."

"Both?"

"Yeah, she kinda insisted. Said she just wanted to get away for a while and that was the easiest way."

"And did she also say it was alright to take advantage of her while she was on her vacation?"

"Well, not in so many words, but it was assumed."

Jerome felt his rage about to explode. He forced it under control. "You got any more?"

"Yeah, but are you gonna let us take our turns?"

"Depends on what you got."

The man hurried forward. "I got a little of both left, but if I give some up, it means I'm next, right?"

Jerome motioned the man forward. As he offered a hand with two pills and a small baggie of meth, Jerome reached forward as if to take them, then jammed the knife into the man's groin and lifted with all his strength. The skin parted like Jell-O. He screamed, eyes bulging at his exposed innards. He clutched at his body to hold everything together, then collapsed to the ground. The line broke and men scattered. He waited. When he was sure no one was lurking to sneak up behind him, he turned and looked for Merri's discarded clothes.

He found them strewn around the alley. They were filthy and smelled, but he wasn't taking her out of there naked. Her skin was so pale and cold he had to check her pulse to see if she was still breathing. He slid pants and a ragged shirt on her, foregoing the bra and panties as too far gone. Then he hoisted her in his arms. Her body was heavy like a dead body. Her head lolled back and her arms hung slack. She mumbled though none of it was coherent except for two words, "My boat."

He carried her down the street where he had hidden his bike and set her on the seat, then slid in behind her. She was too boneless to keep upright, and he needed both hands to ride. He remembered passing a men's clothing store. He set Merri down on the ground, propped up against the brick wall, then walked back to the shop. As yet, no one had broken in, perhaps thinking there was nothing of value to loot. Food and water were more important than clothes.

He picked up a decorative brick from around a tree near the street and heaved it through the glass front door. It did not shatter. Instead, the glass webbed but held together. Jerome used the brick to pound an opening large enough to slip his hand through and unlocked the latch.

Once inside, Jerome found two of the largest leather belts he could find, then looked for something that might fit Merri. Though tall, she had a slim frame. He settled on T-shirts and the smallest size package of briefs. As an afterthought, he found a small water-repellent jacket, then went out.

Merri had slumped to the side and now lay with her head on the concrete. He slipped her old, stained T-shirt off and worked a new one on, then slid her arms into the jacket. He stowed the briefs for when she was conscious, whenever that might be. This time, when he had her situated on the bike, he joined the belts, wrapped them around his body then fastened them in front of Merri, holding her upright and bound to him.

He took the trip back to Sarge's place slowly, not wanting to upend the delicate balance between bike and riders.

He was forced to turn his head from Merri's as the stench rising from her unkempt body caused his eyes to water. As they rode, he allowed his thoughts to drift to more memorable times with Merri.

Merri was in the Coast Guard and stationed in Chicago. She achieved the rank of Chief Petty Officer, which placed her above the enlisted ranks but subordinate to the commissioned officers. Though she bridged the gap between the two groups, her main function was to serve as a technical expert, providing insight and advice to commissioned officers.

When Jerome first met Merri, she was pushing herself to be offered command of one of the smaller vessels assigned to the Chicago station. After being given the opportunity once, she wanted more. She was driven to improve her skills to prove her capabilities to the ranks beneath her as well as the officers.

She was taking one of the martial arts classes he was then teaching. He was impressed by her drive, intensity, endurance, and willingness to push beyond her limits. Recognizing a kindred spirit, he began offering extra after-class training sessions, which eventually led to a brief but intense relationship.

She stopped coming around when a male counterpart was offered command of the vessel she had her sights on. Feeling slighted, she fell into a depression which was where she was the last time he saw her. That was two weeks before the pandemic hit. It was obvious now that her spiral had continued. This was about as rock bottom as a person could go.

When he pulled up in front of Sarge's apartment building, he was surprised to see a delivery van parked on the sidewalk in front of the doors. Sarge had taken it upon himself to secure a ride. It was the type used to make home deliveries and had ample room for Sarge's belongings. It was an excellent choice. It offered room to haul and space to sleep.

He checked Merri's pulse to make sure she was still alive. He had no idea how much of the two drugs she took, but if she slipped into a coma, he doubted she'd ever come out.

Sarge exited the door and spotted Merri. An instant snarl rose to his lips. He had no patience or acceptance for those who would throw away God's gifts, especially those who destroyed their bodies and minds with drugs.

"What's she doing here?"

"She's coming."

"She must be riding with you then."

"Come on, Sarge. She's one of us."

"She might have been, but she's since thrown it all away."

"You gonna turn your back on a sister in need. She's a good person. If I can salvage her, I will. Please, don't fight me on this. She needs help."

"What if she refuses to accept it?"

"That's on her. All we can do is try."

"You gonna be willing to give up on her if she doesn't respond?"

Jerome sighed and studied the near comatose woman. "Yeah. If it comes to that, we leave her on her own."

"As long as we're understood. It's going to be hard enough out there as it is. Put her in the back."

"Thanks, Sarge."

He laid Merri down and placed the package of briefs under her head for a pillow. "How much longer you need?"

"One more trip will do. You give any thought to where you want to go?"

"Not really."

"Well, I've got some ideas on that. I'll tell you when I come back."

"You want me to help?"

"No. You stay with the van. Wouldn't make sense to do all this work just to have some low life steal it."

Chapter Twelve

Thirty minutes later, Sarge closed the rear doors and turned to Jerome. "You ready to hear my idea?"

Jerome laughed. "Sure, Sarge. What-chu got?"

"Now, hear me out on this. I think we should meet up with your friend and listen to what he has to say. I want to know more. We can make a final decision after that, but if there's a threat to our national security, we took an oath to defend this country against all attackers, be they foreign or domestic. I'm thinking if this is real, we should do our part."

Jerome wasn't surprised. Sarge was the ultimate patriot, but that didn't mean it was the smart thing to do. "You realize that the threat to our national security has already happened and can't be countered, right?"

"Wrong. The initial attack has been launched, but there are still American citizens that need protecting."

"I thought you didn't believe in conspiracy theories."

"I don't, but I also been around long enough to know anything is possible. If there's a chance this story, no matter how farfetched, is true, then I want to learn more and be a part of the solution."

Jerome was unconvinced and was about to list his reasons when a large delivery truck rounded the corner and honked at them. In seconds, Sarge and Jerome had their hands filled with a gun and found defensive positions around the van.

The truck stopped twenty yards away and Moore leaned out the passenger window and said, "I heard there's a party here. Thought we might join."

Jerome's jaw sagged. As Sarge broke cover and advanced toward the truck, he placed a finger under Jerome's chin and pushed his mouth closed. Sarge had met Moore on occasion and they shared a mutual respect.

"Join us where?" Jerome asked. "We haven't decided where we're going yet."

"Yes, you have," Moore and Sarge said at the same time. Moore reached through the window and fist-bumped Sarge.

"We know you better than you know yourself," Moore said.

"Got that right," said Sarge. "I could see it in your eyes. If this is a conspiracy, the thought lit a fire inside you. At the very least, we need more information, and the only way to get that is to join this Weatherman friend of yours."

"Oh yeah," Moore said. "I'd go if only to meet this legend, but Sarge is right. We all signed on for an ideal. To serve and protect this nation. If there're people out there responsible for the deaths of American people on such a grand scale, then it's our duty to respond."

Though he started on a light note, by the end, Moore had his own fire glinting in his eyes. It was out of character. He was not one to get involved unless it benefitted him. Jerome wondered if there was more to the man's desire to leave than he was stating.

"Mount up," Sarge said. "You know we're right."

"Well, since you all know me so well."

"Hey, where we going?" asked Moore.

"South, down I-90."

The truck pulled away from the curb as Jerome sat on his bike. "You don't want me to lead?" Jerome asked.

"Are you kidding? You know who you're talking to? I'm a Ranger. Rangers lead the way." He slipped the tan beret worn by the 2nd battalion of the 75th regiment on his bald dome and the truck sped away.

Jerome revved the bike to life and pulled out next, leaving Sarge to bring up the rear. He had no idea what they were getting into, but Sarge and Moore were right. Deep inside, he knew this was always his plan. The thought of riding off away from the brewing conflict had appeal and was sure to be the safer choice, but running from a fight was not in his nature, especially if he could make a difference.

They hit the I-90 expressway and twenty minutes later, the city of Chicago was fading in his mirror. Now they just had to figure out how to find Weatherman and his people. He had a basic idea of where to look, but knowing Weatherman as he did, he just had to follow the bodies.

They moved from I-90 to I-94, and when that branched, they went west, connecting with I-294. From there, they hit a cloverleaf and went south on Route One. The directions Weatherman had given him were a little iffy from that point. Jerome pulled to the front of the small convoy and signaled to pull over.

"What's up?" Moore asked, jumping down from the seat. He tossed an apple to Jerome, then stretched his long legs and twisted his trunk.

Sarge came up to join them. Moore handed him an apple. The older man slid it into a pocket.

Jerome finished chewing and then said, "From here, the directions aren't clear. He told me to keep heading south until we hit farmland, then east until we saw something that left no doubt it was them."

"Seriously? That's it?" Moore said. "Could he be any more cryptic?"

"I got the feeling it was something a military person might know about but perhaps think it out of place."

"You mean like a tank or something?" asked Moore.

"Maybe. He gave me one other thing. It was a farm somewhere close to Goodenow Road. We head south until we hit Goodenow, then go east."

"But we have no idea how far that is?" Moore asked.

"None. Anyone got a map?"

They looked at Sarge, who grunted. "Of course, I do. Young people are never prepared." He strode away, grumbling to himself. When he returned, he had a paper map of Illinois spread out. He found the area and folded the map into a square, then held it so they could all see.

With a finger, he traced their path until they turned off I-294. He glanced up, looked around, then held a finger on a spot. "We're here." He ran his finger down Route One. "It connects with Main Street in Steger, then continues as Route One. We keep going until One ends at three ninety-four."

Moore stabbed at the map with a forefinger to Sarge's annoyance. "There it is. Goodenow."

"Yes," Sarge said, pulling the map away from Moore's long finger. "Goodenow does not appear to be very long."

"It's definitely farmland," Jerome said. "I'm betting they're in one of those farmhouses. I should mention that we're entering hostile territory and should be on alert."

"How we gonna know the good guys from the bad?"

"From the little I know, the bad guys might be wearing some sort of military uniform."

"No black hats?" Moore joked.

"We've got a direction now," Sarge said, interrupting. "Let's move out."

Moore looked at Jerome and laughed. "I think we got us a trail boss here."

"Does sound like it," said Jerome.

"Boss, yes," Sarge said, "But I'd never let either of you two clowns join my wagon train."

As Moore started back to the truck, Jerome said, "How's she doing?"

Sarge shook his head. "Nothing so far."

"Did you check to see if she was still breathing?"

"I did. She is. You sure she's worth trying to save? If she wakes, she's gonna be in bad shape."

"She's still a person and beyond that, she was military, like us. Never leave 'em behind."

Sarge nodded. "Well, she stinks. Had to put up two air fresheners."

"Wait, you brought air fresheners?"

Sarge shook his head and mumbled, "Young people, never prepared," as he went back to the van.

They drove for another twenty minutes at a slower speed to ensure they didn't run into an ambush. As they neared the Village of Crete, Jerome circled back to the van and rode alongside. Sarge leaned out the window to hear. "I'm going to ride ahead a bit to scout. Keep this pace and this route. If I'm not back in twenty minutes, get off this road and hide. If I can, I'll find you."

"How will you do that?"

"Leave me a sign."

He rode off and was quickly out of sight as the curves in the road and buildings obscured him. He checked side streets and timed out ten minutes reaching the southern side of Crete before stopping. The road ahead was straight. Though he could see a long way, he dug through his bag and withdrew small but powerful binoculars. He scanned ahead, then panned right to left in a slow arc. On the return pass, movement flicked ahead. A vehicle drove from east to west across Route One. Though it was a mere second of a glimpse, he was certain it was a military-style Humvee.

With the glasses focused down the road, he wondered what the sight meant. Were they friend or foe? Part of Weatherman's people or the enemy? Weatherman had arrived in ACU pants and a T-shirt but was driving a minivan. If he had access to a Humvee, Jerome doubted he'd be driving a soccer mom vehicle. That meant the enemy was patrolling the streets.

He was about to turn back when another vehicle, this one an open jeep with a mounted fifty caliber machine gun in back, turned toward him. This was no time to discover their allegiance. He swung the bike around and sped back the way he came. Once in the village and blocked from view, he thought about taking an alternate course to lead them away from the others but decided against it. If his friends didn't see him soon, they might continue right into the advancing jeep.

He opened the throttle to max and less than a minute later, spotted the truck. He slowed and motioned for Moore's friend to turn. He could see her glance at Moore. Jerome waved with more emphasis and Moore had her make the turn. They went west on Cass Street until it made a northern turn. Two blocks later, Jerome motioned for them to pull behind the Crete Village Hall.

Jerome called to them, "Shut them down," then drove across the street and parked behind a bakery off the road and out of view. If the occupants of the jeep searched the area, it was alright to find the bike, but the others would be safe.

He ran between the truck and van. Moore and Sarge had their windows down. "Spotted a weaponized military jeep. There's a good chance they spotted me. Until we can determine friend from foe, I thought it best to keep out of sight. Stay inside and be ready. I'm going to scout."

Jerome scaled the truck's hood, then went up to the roof. From there, he took a running start and leaped for the roof of the building. He landed in a crouch, then moved toward the front and laid down. With the glasses trained between the buildings, he found angles that gave him a view of the main road. Less than a minute later, the jeep flew past his first line of sight. He followed its progress under an overpass, which blocked further viewing.

How long would they follow before giving up? Would they come back and search or head back to wherever their base was? How long should they wait before moving? All good questions with no answers. However, the equation changed with the arrival of another jeep and a Humvee. They drove into Crete but did not exit. The vehicles stopped on Main Street behind a row of buildings. Jerome had no idea what they were doing.

He was about to move to a different position when the first jeep returned. This one he could see when it stopped. A discussion ensued, then the jeep turned east into the residential streets of Crete. The other two vehicles moved forward and turned west directly toward them.

Chapter Thirteen

Jerome scooted back from the edge and ran in a crouch to the rear. "Hey!" he called, "They're coming. The others scrambled deeper inside the vehicles while he debated whether to jump down or keep to higher ground. The sound of the engine approaching decided for him. He crawled back and lay prone. Their hiding place was only two short blocks from the main road. It wouldn't take long for them to search and leave.

The jeep came down the road between the Village Hall and the police department. Two men were inside, both scanning the area. The driver started to turn left away from them when the passenger said something. The passenger eyed the truck.

"What's the problem?" the driver asked.

"I led the team that searched this village two days ago. We stripped the police station there." He pointed at the building across from the hall.

"Yeah, so?"

"I don't remember that truck being there."

The two men studied the truck. Then the passenger motioned the driver to turn right. They crawled along until they were behind Moore's vehicle. With the van revealed, the passenger said, "That van's new too."

"You think they're with the motorcycle guy?"

"Makes sense. Maybe he's their scout."

The Humvee came around the far corner and moved alongside the jeep. After a brief discussion, the passenger climbed out, pulling a sidearm from a holster. The side door of the Humvee opened, spitting out three well-armed soldiers. Though they were obviously military-trained,

Jerome did not recognize the insignias on their ACUs. Was this the group Weatherman spoke of—the militia?

They spread out and aimed their M-16s at the van and the truck. In his haste, Sarge had left his window down. The passenger appeared to be the man in charge and angled toward the window with his gun raised. He did a quick peek inside, then took a longer look. "You in the van, come out now with your hands empty, or I will instruct my men to fire. The walls of this van do not have the stopping power for you to survive. Come out now."

As he spoke, the driver of the jeep climbed up behind the fifty cal and turned the long barrel toward the van.

Nothing happened for a moment. Then the leader said, "On my command, men, hose this vehicle down."

Jerome had a shot at two of the five threats, including the man behind the fifty cal. Though he only had a handgun, he was a good enough shot to take either of them down, but the machine gun was the greater threat, so he took aim at him and waited.

"Okay. Okay, don't shoot. I'm coming. I'm an old man, so give me a moment."

"If I see a gun, we will fire."

"Okay. I'm coming out without a weapon."

Jerome could see the van rocking. Then he noticed Moore had crept to the cab and was checking the outside mirror. He ducked below the window level and peered up to see Jerome. Moore flipped flopped his hand to indicate he wanted to know if something was safe.

The van door swung wide and Sarge struggled to get out using his cane.

The leader said, "I said no weapons."

"I ain't got no weapon," Sarge said, his voice sounding feeble.

"What's that cane?"

"Oh, that? I can't walk without it. Like I said, I'm an old man."

With all eyes focused on Sarge, Jerome flashed fingers and nodded it was safe for whatever Moore was going to do.

Sarge reached the ground and held onto the door for support. "Okay. I'm out. I'm no threat to you or your men."

"What's that symbol on your cane?" The leader asked, referring to the round golden ball on the top end. "Is that the Marine Corp symbol?"

"It is."

"Hey, boys, we got us a real live Marine here."

The men responded with grunts and seemed to relax a bit. While they were distracted, Moore cracked the passenger door and slid his long frame to the ground. He hurried forward and squatted behind the tandem rear wheels. The Asian woman followed him out and slid behind the front tires. Then she disappeared around the front of the truck.

The leader said, "Anyone else inside?"

"No, sir. It's just me."

"It is, huh? You got a guy riding a motorcycle with you?"

"No, Sir, but I did see one pass me on my way here. He tore past me so fast I barely had a chance to notice if he's a man or woman."

"We're going to search the van, so if anyone's inside, it's best you tell me now."

"Nope. No one, Sir."

"Okay, then we're confiscating your van and everything inside."

"What? No! Why you gonna take everything I got?"

"Cause I can."

"Under what authority?"

The man laughed. "Don't need any authority, but if it makes you feel better, it's being confiscated by the new American militia serving under the new government."

"There ain't no such thing, and from what I've seen, there ain't no government either."

"This is going to happen with or without you being alive."

A low moan came from the back of the van. Jerome winced. Of all the times for Merri to regain consciousness. If Jerome heard it perched on the roof, he knew the soldiers did, too. By their reaction, they had.

The two men near the rear aimed their weapons at the double doors. The leader pointed his gun at Sarge. "I thought you said there wasn't anyone else inside."

"It's just a druggie I found on the side of the road. Hell, I wasn't even sure if she was alive."

"Yet you put her in your van anyway. You been having sex with a corpse? Is that it, you sick twisted bastard?"

"No, Sir." He sounded nervous, but Jerome knew Sarge was anything but afraid.

"You keep an eye on him," the leader told the third man who was out of Jerome's line of sight. Sarge would have to deal with him.

"Open those doors and come out of there," the leader said.

"Sir, she's probably not conscious."

"Dexter, open that door."

The man moved to the doors and reached for the handle, but before he made contact, both doors flew open. The one door hit the man, taking him by surprise and knocking him a step backward. Before he could regain his balance or anyone could move, a steady barrage of shots came from inside.

The soldier standing back from the doors took multiple rounds and dropped. The off-balance man lifted his weapon but never got the chance to fire before Jerome sent rounds tearing through his face.

Moore stood and emptied half a thirty-round mag from his B&T APC9k submachine pistol into the gunner in the jeep. With his target down, Jerome swung his focus to the leader, but before he could pull the trigger, the Asian woman rose from behind the van where she had moved and triggered a round into the man's forehead.

A second later, Sarge emerged from the far side of the van, his opponent dispatched.

The driver of the Humvee pressed the gas pedal down and the vehicle shot forward. That direction offered no outlet and he was forced to make a wide turn in the parking lot across the street. To escape, he had to run back past the shooters. The heavy body and protective glass held up to the assault of nine-millimeter rounds. The steady pounding from the SMG eventually punched holes through the windshield, but none struck the driver, who managed to get away. He vanished around the corner.

By the time Jerome climbed down from the roof, Moore and his friend were stripping the bodies.

Merri had crawled out of the van and was doubled over vomiting. She almost fell over until Sarge grabbed her hips from behind to give her support. When she was done, she straightened to a slight bend and looked around.

Moore looked up from his work and smiled. "First kill?"

"Today," Merri said and retched again. She wiped her mouth with the back of her hand and groaned as she clutched her stomach. "Who are you people and how did I get here?"

Jerome stood in front of her. "You alright, Merri?"

From a doubled over position, she craned her neck to look up. "Jerome, is that you?"

"Yeah."

"Where am I? Why does my cooch hurt? What the hell did you do to me?"

"Oh, no. You did anything you're feeling to yourself. Looks like you been on a self-destructive path for a while."

"I don't feel good."

"And it's gonna get worse before it gets better. We don't have time for you to be sick. We need to go before others come looking."

"Were there others with them?" Moore asked.

"Yeah, another jeep."

"Maybe we should take the fifty cal with us."

"Don't have time to take it apart, but if you want it, drive it. We don't have the luxury of numbers, so decide and let's go." Jerome helped Merri climb into the back of the van. She lay down with a moan and curled into a ball. He closed the doors and ran across the street for his bike.

When he returned, Sarge had the map out. "Down the road to Exchange then turn left. Let's get out of the area and I'll direct you from there."

"You lead."

Sarge backed the van out. Jerome motioned for the Asian woman whom Moore still hadn't introduced to follow, and he brought up the rear. As they drove, Jerome wondered about the choice he made, joining Weatherman's little war, especially now that they had their first skirmish. They reached the turn without further complications, but how long would it take for the enemy who had identified themselves as members of the new American militia to come in pursuit? If this were truly an army, what troops and equipment could they bring to bear upon them?

Only time would tell. With luck, they'd join with Weatherman before the next encounter and maybe get some answers.

Part 2

Chapter Fourteen

Ellie watched the camp, studying the movements and patterns. By the time she had returned from leaving the signals and message for Weatherman, it was dark and the camp had gone still. Long Shot still sat in the middle of the grounds, but now Astronaut was back. He was lying down and didn't look capable of moving. If he was that severely injured, it made escape more improbable.

With the camp asleep except for the four guards stationed on the buildings at each corner of the base, she had room to maneuver in the dark. She wished there was a way to get to the guards but climbing a metal building without making noise was outside her skill set. Still, she was on fire with pulsing adrenaline after her most recent kill of the drunk man who wanted to party with her.

The thought of taking one of these soldiers with a knife was exhilarating. *No! Focus. Long Shot and Astronaut need you.* She narrowed her gaze and plotted her moves. Ellie was sure she could reach the first building unseen. She had the guards' pattern memorized. If the guard to the left didn't make a sudden turn, reaching the outer building was easy.

She closed her eyes to visualize the camp. The trees came to within twenty feet of the road that circled the camp. Ten feet beyond that was a long narrow building that ran north and south. On the other side of that were four larger buildings running east and west. They stood a little taller than the narrow building giving them more reach for distance, but the guard's view was hindered once she got behind the first building. She had to cross another road that ran between the four taller constructions and the narrow building.

Past the four buildings was open ground in the shape of an oval football field. To the right was a small road that connected to the street. On the other side of that was a large pond. From the buildings in front of her to the six buildings that lined the opposite side near the street was a stretch of fifty yards of open ground. The chopper was parked across the field near the first building closest to the street. Long Shot and Astronaut were on the ground almost midway between the two sets of buildings in clear view of all four guards. However, their focus looked to be directed more outward than toward the middle.

Sure of her mental map, Ellie sucked in a deep breath and corralled her racing nerves. When the two closest guards had their backs to her, she darted from concealment. She ran across the open space in a crouch. Her feet kicked gravel that skittered across the narrow road. The guard on the right began to turn as she reached the safety of the outer building.

She checked her breathing to keep from gasping for air and heard the guard call to the other one, "Did you hear something?"

The silence before the response increased her angst. What was she doing? She didn't have the skill to do this stealth stuff. This was stupid and she was going to get killed. And for what?

"Nah! I haven't heard anything all night."

Courage and confidence returned. *To save her new friends. That's what.*

She waited five minutes before moving, then went left toward the guard on the left. She feared going right.

Another noise might make him suspicious. Ellie moved to the far end of the narrow building and peered around. The guard to her left was moving away from her, so she rounded the corner and moved forward. The guard to her right was heading toward her. She ducked back. If the other guard made a turn and came back, she was in the open. Though night had fallen, there was enough ambient light from the stars to make her visible.

Wait or retreat? She froze. She had to decide, but her mind was locked up with fear. As the guard made his turn, she forced herself to move. She darted forward without looking and made it between the third and fourth east-west buildings. She had no idea where the guard to her right was when she made the move. No alarm sounded. Had she gone unseen, or was he silently stalking her?

She waited, realizing her breaths were loud and ragged. She had to remain calm or this mission would fail. Listen to her, talking about missions like she was a real soldier. No, what did the man called Money say? Tier two operatives? Yes, she liked that. Though terrified, she had to admit she had never felt more alive. She got down on her knees and crawled to the end of the building. How did they do it while carrying this long rifle? She held it off the ground with one hand and crawled on her knees with the other hand. The going was slow. She had no idea if anyone was inside the building. It didn't matter. Her concern was the four guards that might see her.

She checked the position of the two across from her. The dim but natural overhead lights of the sliver moon as she called it, and the stars were enough to make out the silhouettes of the two men on the buildings. She no longer had eyes on the other two. Then, she located the two dark forms on the grass twenty-five yards away. They were off to her right, which made the dash to reach them longer.

She strained to see better but thought the two lumps moved. She waited. Minutes later, they moved again. Only she noticed it wasn't both moving. One was dragging the other. She was unable to determine which one was doing the work, but it made no difference. They were shortening the distance between her and them if only a few feet at a time.

Ellie wanted to get more in line with their position, so she crawled backward. When the way was clear, she moved around the corner but decided the rifle was too much of a nuisance to carry. She set it down in the grass at the end of the third building, then ducked and crawled forward between the second and third structures. She lay still and watched. Little by little, the two men edged closer to her position. She wanted to signal the awake one to make him aware of her presence but feared she might draw attention to them. She cheered silently every time they made a move.

How long would it be before one of the guards noticed their altered position? How could she help them? The next move brought them to within twenty yards, however, she realized now that they were angling between buildings one and two. She backed up and moved again. She got to the end and started around the corner, then remembered the rifle. After retrieving it, she turned and froze. The guard above her on building one just made his turn. She froze, knowing movement would catch his eye.

His walk to the near end took an eternity. She wanted to raise the rifle and aim but was afraid to move. The guard reached the end and stood there for a moment, his gaze focused outward, not down. After an agonizing minute, he pivoted and started back. She released the breath she had unintentionally been holding and moved forward. The stock of the rifle grazed the corner of the building. She cursed inwardly, squatted, and set the rifle down along the end of the building. At her lowered height, the guard could not see her, but if he heard and came looking, she was in the open. As quietly as she could manage, Ellie duckwalked to the first building and pressed against it. The guard would have to be right above her, looking straight down to see her.

She waited a long while before sliding midway down the building. Her new friends were now but fifteen yards away, going ever so slowly.

"Freeze right there."

She squeaked in surprise, then slapped both hands over her mouth. The guard had heard her and had come down to check on the noise she made. *Stupid amateur!* she chastised.

"Turn around slowly and keep your hands out to the sides."

Petrified, Ellie did as ordered. Her mind raced for a believable cover story.

"Who are you and more importantly, why are you here?"

"Ah, well, this is embarrassing, but I met one of your soldier friends when he was out on patrol earlier today and he suggested I stop by tonight for some fun."

"Ah-ha, and who is this soldier?"

"His name was Doug. He said he was an officer, but I suspect he just told me that so I'd agree to meet him. But it's so dark and there're so many buildings, how am I supposed to find him?"

"Take that gun from the holster and drop it on the ground."

She did. Ellie had to buy time for Long Shot and Astronaut to reach safety. That meant she had to turn the guard around so he didn't catch movement.

"Do you know where I can find Doug?"

"I don't know any Doug."

She took a step forward and stuck out a pouty lip though she wasn't sure he could see it. "So, you can't help me? Maybe you can point me to an officer. I do love a man in charge."

The stern look and harsh tone lightened. "If you just want an officer, I can be a general."

"Oh, I like the way you think. Only I should be the general so you can stand at attention for me."

That brought a smile, and she took advantage by moving closer.

"Since I can't find Doug and I came all this way, maybe you'd like to show me a good time, General. What are your orders?"

Ellie moved again, this time angling away from him. She didn't stop but walked past him, trailing a finger across his chest.

"Oh, that felt really hard. Tell me, are all your muscles that—hard?" She said the word in a breathy deductive fashion.

As hoped, he turned with her. With his back to the field, her friends could move without being seen, at least by him. She just had to keep him occupied until they arrived. The question was, how far was she willing to go to help them? She wasn't necessarily opposed to getting naked for the man, however, sex was a different matter. Though it didn't bother her to display her body to him, she had a strange reluctance to allow Long Shot or Astronaut a look. Perhaps because she didn't want them to think less of her even though her actions were only to help them escape.

She moved to the rear of the building and pressed her back against the wall. The shadows were deeper here, which buoyed her confidence and resolve. Whatever happened, she was going to make sure this man did not stop her friends.

He rounded on her and let his eyes travel her body. "Are you really here to see someone named Doug?"

She stretched the neck of her shirt down, exposing her cleavage, then drew a cross over her breast. "Cross my heart. At least, I think he said his name was Doug. Might have been Dave."

Chapter Fifteen

The man smiled and moved closer. She released the neckline, which caused a small groan of protest from the guard as her chest was recovered. He pressed tight to her and ground his hips into her. "Oh, someone is at attention and wants a salute."

He moved his head and smashed his lips into hers, rocking her head back against the metal wall of the building. She hit hard enough to cause tears. She almost cried out in anger and had to stop herself from biting his tongue off. Instead, she allowed him to explore her mouth. She wrapped her hands around his head and kept him close, kissing him deeper and with more heat.

He slid his rifle behind him and it hung from the sling. As one hand gripped her hair while the other descended and the fondling began. He was rough and had no finesse. She was sure he was nothing more than a wham, bang, thank, you ma'am, kind of guy though most likely without the thank you. She had to make sure whatever they did lasted long enough for her friends to reach safety. From there, well, she still had the pocketknife she made her first kill with. Though if she allowed her pants to come off, she might not be able to reach the weapon.

She tried to slow him down, but his actions were insistent, and he muscled her to a pinned position. He had her breasts out and in his mouth much sooner than she wanted, not bothering to disrobe her, just pulling her shirt and bra up. He began fumbling with her belt, but she pulled him tight and bit his ear lobe, then planted a huge bite on his neck. From the low moan he was making, she knew she had him electrified.

She placed her hands inside the folds of his shirt and pulled. Though she managed to separate two buttons from the buttonholes, the shirt was well made and resisted. He snared her hands and pushed them against the building. "My shirt stays on in case I get called to duty. In fact, all my clothes stay on, but it's time for yours to come off," she breathed.

The much larger man pushed his forearm under her chin to keep her in place. It was tight against her throat. She gasped for air and experienced desperate panic. "I don't think you came here to see anyone." His free hand unbuckled her belt. "I think you're here to cause trouble. I'm going to inflict internal damage, and when I'm done, I'm going to take you to someone who will inflict external damage."

He opened her pants and pulled them apart. Then he dropped his forearm and slammed a shoulder into her, holding her in place while he gripped and yanked her pants and panties down to her knees.

With his head near her chin, she bit his ear hard. He pulled away, put a hand to his ear, then checked his fingers. Blood. She smiled. "You bitch!" He slapped her, then fumbled his erection free while holding her still with one meaty hand on her chest.

He tried to push in, but she kept her thighs tight. That angered him as his frustration grew. He pulled her away from the building, then slammed her back. The noise was loud, and he flinched and looked around.

"You spread, or I'm going to hurt you."

"Maybe I don't want to do it standing up, big boy. You want to slam me, take me from behind. Let me get on the ground and I'll take my pants off. Then you can ride me all night or the thirty seconds I expect it to be."

He dropped his hand. "Do it."

She bent, but as she squatted, he grabbed the back of her head and pushed her toward his crotch. If he was dumb enough to allow her mouth that close, he was in for a world of pain. The only problem was the noise he'd make. He must have thought the same thing and shoved her away. However, it did give her the cover she needed to withdraw the knife from her pocket.

"Hurry up," he commanded. She smiled up at him and slid one leg free from her pants. She started to get on her knees, then stopped and rolled to her back. Her legs parted, giving him a full and open invitation. It was more than his self-control could manage. He dropped, aimed, and plunged. She gasped at first as the rough entry ignited pain, but it gave her cover to open the knife. She ignored his thrusts as he pounded violently into her. She knew he wouldn't last long and didn't want him to finish.

Ellie jammed the knife into the side of the man's well-muscled neck and yanked with all her strength. He pulled back, a look of astonishment on his face. As she severed the artery and the blood gushed, spraying the wall, the look changed to panic. As he pulled back, she wrapped her legs tightly around him to keep him in place. He flopped out of her and she snagged the now flaccid penis, tugged, and sliced through it before he realized what was happening.

She unwound her legs, pulled them up, and slammed them into his chest, toppling him over. He was trying to scream, to call for help, but she dove on him and when his mouth opened, she shoved what was left of his manhood inside, further gagging him. She then lay on top of him as he squirmed and pressed her palms over his mouth. He rolled to dislodge her, but she extended her legs to the side to keep her balance and rode him like he had hoped to do to her until he no longer thrashed. He died with his eyes open and his mouth full. She planted a kiss on his forehead. "I hate to say it, but it was much better for me than it was for you."

She wiped her bloody hands on his shirt, then gathered her pants and dressed quickly. Then she rolled the body against the wall. As she peered around the corner to see the progress Long Shot and Astronaut had made, she found they had just arrived between the buildings.

Ellie hurried forward and grabbed Astronaut's other arm. Her sudden appearance shocked an exclamation from Long Shot. "Shh! It's me, Ellie."

Relief shown in his eyes. He stood and the two of them dragged Astronaut behind the buildings.

"God am I happy to see—" He stopped when he spotted the body.

"Can you hold him?" Ellie asked.

Long Shot nodded.

She let Astronaut go and then grabbed the discarded rifle and handgun. After positioning to hold him alone, she said, "Get the guard's weapons." She struggled to hold him erect but didn't have to for long. Once Long Shot returned, they moved, dragging Astronaut between them.

They rounded the long narrow building and were now blocked from the guard's view across the grounds. However, the guard to the far end still had a clear line of sight. They waited until he turned his back, then hustled across the open ground toward the shadows of the trees. They hadn't gone more than ten feet into the trees when they heard a voice shout, "Hey! Where are the prisoners?"

They hurried as best they could to get distance from the camp. Ellie was sure it would be obvious which direction they went, especially once they discovered the dead guard.

Long Shot said, "They'll be coming soon. They'll organize for a minute, then be on our trail. Once they find the guard you killed, they'll have a good idea of our direction. We won't be able to outrun them, so you keep going with him and I'll buy you time."

"I'm not sure I can drag him very far."

"Get as far away as possible. Angle away from this path. In the dark, it will take time for them to pick up your trail. I'll keep them off you. If you can't keep going, then find someplace to hide."

They kept going another five minutes. Ellie did her best to keep up with Long Shot, but she just wasn't as strong or in as good of shape. Her breathing came in painful gasps through a harsh throat.

"Okay, I hear them coming. You have about a five-minute head start, but that will evaporate fast. Take him, and please, keep him safe." He let go and she instantly felt the extra burden. "And Ellie, thank you for coming for us."

"Of course. We're a team."

He turned to find a shooting spot while Ellie wrapped Astronaut tightly and dragged him. Her progress was as slow as it felt. She turned northeast. In the dark, she stumbled twice and fell once. She stayed where she fell for a moment, thinking it was as far as she could go, but when she heard Astronaut moan, it gave her new hope that he might wake any second. She bent, grabbed him under the arms, and dragged him, moving backward. She lasted two more minutes, but when her heel caught on an exposed, raised root, she fell, and this time stayed down. Astronaut did not recover as hoped, but after two falls she might have knocked him out again. She tried to catch her breath, and if she wasn't going to keep moving, she had to find a place to hide in the deep, dark shadows, but she was too exhausted.

The first shot pierced the night a minute later and her break was over. As the intensity of the gunfight increased, she hauled Astronaut up and started moving again. Two minutes later, the last shot was fired and Ellie began to worry that Long Shot was dead. If so, it was time to find a place to hide.

She spied a dark mound to her left and dragged Astronaut toward it. It was a thicket of vines and brush. She moved around the back of the ten-foot-wide area and set Astronaut down. It took several tries and a lot of scratches to part the vines enough to squeeze through. Then she reached back, latched onto Astronaut, and pulled him in behind her.

Once inside, she pulled the rifle from her shoulder, then the handgun from the holster. She was ready for battle. Ellie, tier two operator. She liked the sound of that.

Chapter Sixteen

Weatherman spotted a scrap of red material fluttering in the breeze along the side of the road before he noticed the body. To be fair, the sun was almost set, so his vision was hindered. At least that was the excuse he gave for the sudden swerve to avoid hitting the body. He pulled to a stop. Money had been dozing in the back seat while Rose had been staring out the side window, lost in her thoughts, perhaps thinking about the loss of the woman she had lived with before the Georgia State Militia had come to recruit her.

Money was thrown forward, prevented from being pitched to the floor only by quick reflexes. To the credit of his training, he came up with gun in hand and head swiveling to acquire a target.

"My bad," Weatherman said. "I think we were just given a signal."

"Signal?" Money said.

Rose noticed it immediately and pointed through the windshield. "The red flag."

"Exactly." He opened the door and unfolded his large frame from the seat. The others followed, all leveling weapons and scanning the surroundings.

Satisfied they were alone and the body wasn't a trap, Weatherman moved to the body while the others covered him. He surveyed the empty building across the street. It appeared abandoned, but it was a good place for an ambush. He trained the gun toward the building as he bent to examine the body. The man was dead. Looked like from multiple stab wounds. It wasn't a kill Long Shot or Astronaut would have done. This was an amateur's kill.

Ellie? Still, there was no doubt about the signal. He counted four flags. Red was a warning. Did that mean his friends were in trouble or that he was riding into it? The addition of the body in the middle of the road sealed the deal. It was obvious the body had been placed there for a reason. A blood smear trail ran from the side of the road to where it lay now. It had been placed there for a purpose.

He studied the building. Something was taped to the door. He motioned he was checking it out and Rose took a covering position while Money watched the opposite side. He approached with caution, still expecting a trap. When he reached the concrete steps leading to the door, he paused and searched the inside for movement. When none came, he climbed to the door and tried to open it. It swung outward. The paper was folded and taped to the glass. He pulled it free and shook the fold. The sheet opened and he read:

Weatherman,
Astronaut and Long Shot captured. Held in camp mile east of here. Antonia dead. Doing surveillance. Will try to rescue if I don't hear from you soon.
Ellie.

Weatherman read it a second time, then turned the sheet over but nothing else was written. He returned to the others and gave his report as he handed the paper to Rose. "Looks like the others have been captured and Ellie is attempting a rescue."

"Oh, God!" Money said.

"Yeah."

Rose said, "Well, I give her credit for trying, but you probably need to find a new girlfriend."

Weatherman frowned.

"Okay," Money said, "We have hostiles close by and friends who need our help. Discussion."

"It would help if we knew how long ago this was left," said Rose. "They could all be dead by now."

"Regardless, we need information. We must locate where they're being held and go from there." Weatherman looked at each of them and got an agreeing nod.

Rose squatted and examined the body. "Blood's congealed but sticky. Hasn't been here too long."

Money said, "Options."

"We drive forward and hide the van," said Rose. "Go on foot from there."

Weatherman said, "If it's truly only a mile, we hide the van here and go all the way on foot. We don't know what assets they may have watching the road."

"We also don't know the captive's condition. If they aren't dead, they may have been tortured. Not that I think they would, but if they broke and gave us away, we may be heading toward an ambush."

"We get off this road, move east, go past the one mile and work our way back."

Again agreement.

"End result," Money said.

"Surveil," Rose said. "We can't do more until we know more."

"But what's the goal. We need an exit strategy for either circumstance."

Weatherman said, "Goal one, rescue and escape. Without a vehicle, we blend into the woods and do what we do best. If they aren't ambulatory, we need a vehicle. That makes mission success more difficult."

"We assess, then decide on what's needed," Money said. "If one goes for a vehicle, it takes a weapon out of the fight. If both need to be assisted, it lessens battle efficiency. It also depends on if a vehicle is available."

"Alright, reassessing, we take the van wide of the area and leave it where we can get to it in case nothing else presents itself. We need to go now before full dark."

With the initial plan established, they slid into the car. Weatherman moved to the trunk and smashed the brake lights. Rose took the interior bulb out and placed it in the glovebox.

They came to the first intersection, West Exchange Street, and turned left. Money focused out the left and rear windows. Rose took the right and front, while Weatherman took the front and left. They moved at mid-range speed to avoid running into an ambush. As they entered the Village of Crete, they slowed. The more buildings along their path, the more chance of being seen or taken by surprise.

At the intersection with Route One they stopped.

"I've got headlights in the distance to the right."

They all looked.

"Will they see us cross?"

"They may see a dark shape but won't know what it is," Rose said.

Weatherman put the van in reverse.

"Hold," Rose said. "They turned east. Same direction we're going."

Money said, "We'll have to be aware."

Weatherman punched the gas and they shot across the intersection. Though dark now, he raced faster than was safe to get ahead of the other vehicle. Three blocks later, Rose said, "I see the cone of their headlights. Speed up and we'll be past them by the next intersection."

Weatherman pushed the pedal to the floor. The four-cylinder engine wasn't made for fast starts and struggled, but the speed increased at a steady pace. He rocked forward and back as if his own body's momentum helped with acceleration.

"I think we're good," Rose said.

Weatherman backed off full speed but still moved fast. They needed to get far enough in front so that when he turned south toward the headlights, they had time to hide the van before going on foot.

They reached three ninety-four and slowed. Weatherman waited for a few seconds before turning right. The road was wider but also had abandoned vehicles in their path which made going fast in the dark problematic. Forced to slow to maneuver, they kept watching ahead for the approaching headlights. The expressway curved west. They were unfamiliar with the road and the area but knew their original base was somewhere nearby.

"Lights," Rose called.

Weatherman braked, shifted into park, and shut the engine off. Money was out the back door and moving toward the median between the east and westbound lanes. Rose went out her door and to the back of the van. Weatherman lay across the front seat keeping his head high enough to see through the windshield.

A hundred yards ahead, a vehicle, Weatherman thought to be a jeep, came to the intersection but did not stop. It disappeared, creating confusion in his mind until he realized the vehicle went under the road. They had no entry to the expressway.

He exited and stood behind the open door watching the far side of the expressway. The taillights of the jeep came into view and grew smaller until they winked out. They hadn't been seen.

Rose whispered from behind the van. "Where'd they go."

"They're gone," Weatherman said. "Must be on patrol as their speed didn't suggest they were hunting."

Money rejoined them. "We have a good idea of where their patrol area is. How much further do you want to go?"

Weatherman looked down the expressway, then back the way they came. "This road offers a good escape route, but it may be too far from where we need to be. If we assume that our friends are still captives, that patrol is not out looking for them. That means, as you say, they have given us information as to the area their base is situated. I say we drive a little closer before going on foot."

The others agreed, and they got back in the van. This time, however, their progress was much slower.

They crept another half mile before seeing headlights in two different directions. Then Rose said, "Over there." She pointed. Ahead and to the right was a bank of lights directed toward the ground. The portable lights were bright and extended high enough to illuminate buildings along the sides with what they assumed to be open ground in between.

"I think we found their base," Rose said.

"Yeah, this is as far as we go," said Weatherman.

Money said, "It's at a lower level than we are. We'll be moving downhill and it looks like we'll have the cover of trees all the way."

"Take what you need," Weatherman said, exiting. "We travel fast and light."

Twenty seconds later, they were on a slope off the side of the expressway heading down toward the enemy base, where they hoped to find their still breathing friends.

Chapter Seventeen

They skirted a pond and worked their way through woods, staying toward the denser areas. They came to three small ponds and traveled their banks, keeping rows of trees between them and the open water. Staying alongside the banks gave them a longer view of what lay ahead. By the time they reached the end of the ponds, that advantage had no benefit.

As they came to a rough dirt road, they squatted to confer. They had seen no signs of a threat in the woods. "The woods are thinning," Weatherman said. "We may be coming to more open ground. "Let's cross this road and move into that thicker section there," he pointed, "and go until we lose cover."

No one offered another option, so they moved. They had just reached the opposite side of the dirt road when they heard a gunshot. They squatted and took cover behind trees. From the echo of the shot, Weatherman was sure it came from a rifle, but who was shooting? Had the soldiers found a new target or had Long Shot and Astronaut escaped? Maybe it was Ellie, which brought up more questions. Was she in trouble, or was she trying to facilitate an escape? Two more individual shots were fired before an answering barrage from automatic weapons. Weatherman formed an image of Long Shot firing the single rounds and the enemy using overwhelming counterforce. Whatever was going on they needed more information which meant they needed to get closer.

Without comment, Weatherman moved. His large form glided easily and with unnatural stealth over the rough, leaf-covered ground. Years of training and jungle survival skills came rushing back. Weapon up and ears focused, listening for sounds that didn't belong in the forest, he advanced until he came to a road. This one was paved and had two lanes.

On the other side, the forest continued. From the sound of the gunfight, the combatants were a hundred yards further and within those trees. He motioned for Rose to cross and go right and pointed Money to the left. He covered them as they crossed, then followed, taking the middle. He had complete confidence in their skills. If there was trouble in these woods, they would find and deal with it.

Movement ahead brought him to a stop. He crouched and slid behind a tree, dropping to one knee. He slid his arm through the sling loop to steady his aim and brought his AR on target. Whoever was heading toward him had no skill in moving through woods at all unless they were severely wounded.

He waited as the noise grew louder, then stopped. Had whoever was coming been made aware of his presence? He didn't see how but silently moved two trees to his left just to be sure. He heard grunts and someone mumbling under their breath followed by a low moan. Heavy trampling gave away the position. He zeroed in on the target. Thirty yards ahead and slightly to the right. He was sure of his aim but not who the target was. He waited. The noise ceased as had the shooting. An eerie silence descended over the woods, an ominous warning as to what might be coming.

He kept his head still but his eyes scanning. A faint rustle of leaves to his right announced a presence. Rose or an enemy? Ahead came more noise. Heavier, trained but not skilled. A man emerged into an open area. He was in standard military combat uniform, which marked him as the enemy. He glanced right as a branch moved. Another soldier came into view. Two more appeared to the right.

They were hunting someone. The person he heard moan? A good bet. Whoever it was had been wounded. If these men were hunting the injured person, that made whoever it was an ally.

Weatherman stayed perfectly still and acquired his target, the first man in the open. He knew Money and Rose were in position and were smart enough to choose targets based on all their positions. Three shots, three kills with one left over. None would assume the others would take him, so they would all shoot. Four down, estimated time, two seconds. Unless threatened, they would wait for his shot.

The man he targeted motioned for the others to move. Two more men followed. The total was six and altered the sequence. They were each responsible for two. Because of the trees, he knew the three of them might not have a shot at the same time, but that wasn't something he could control. They moved to within twenty yards. He was about to fire when he heard a vehicle approaching on the road behind them. Had this been a trap? No, he decided. They wouldn't have put the men in front of them in such imminent danger.

Forced to wait until he knew how the approaching vehicle altered the equation, the targets in front of him moved ever closer. He lowered a hand and gripped his combat knife, ready for a silent kill if the man came closer. Brakes squeaked. The vehicle was stopping. The front man heard it too and stopped. Orders were given from behind. "You two to the right, we'll go left."

'We'll'—more than one. A jeep would hold four. Four plus six was ten. He had to act before the forces behind joined. He broke the trigger—one shot. The target dropped. He swung his aim left and fired twice as the man was already moving for cover—a hit but not a kill.

On his left and right, Money and Rose engaged. He was sure three bodies hit the ground. He moved, diving for the cover of another tree but now laying down and focused on the men coming from the rear. Money and Rose would have done the same. Bullets ripped through branches and leaves above him. His hope was friendly fire would catch the men behind him to even the odds.

He heard a cry of pain and knew one person had been hit. Now, not knowing who they faced, the rear group fired. Neither group had any idea who they were shooting at. The battle was fierce and lasted several minutes before dropping to sporadic fire and then to silence. No one was ready to move. In the dark, noise equaled a target.

A low moan came from the front. A leaf crunched from behind. The leaf cruncher panicked and ran hard to Weatherman's left. He tracked him but did not fire. Seconds later, the sound of a struggle ended quickly. Rose, he thought. One more down. He ran the numbers, three down on the initial exchange, two to three wounded. One more down behind and one wounded. Five to six actives in front, two in back. Conclusion, eliminate the lesser group.

He marked his next cover, then assessed the ground in front of him with his hand. With care, he moved two leaves, then placed his knees with caution before moving his hands. It took a full minute to move the three feet to the next tree. He stopped there to listen.

Behind him he heard someone move. It was fast and short. Someone was running from one tree to another. It happened twice more. They were closing the gap. He repeated his process, moving faster than he liked timing it with the movement of another soldier behind him. A muffled grunt followed. Then a voice, "Lezcano. Call out."

If Lezcano could call out, he was smart enough not to. His lack of response told Weatherman Money made sure he was unable to do so.

A voice called from behind him, "Corporal Waters, is that you?"

"LT?" the front man answered.

"Jesus Christ, have we been shooting at each other?"

The fool Lieutenant stood and began moving toward Weatherman, no longer concerned about danger. He passed within three feet. As silent as a shadow, Weatherman rose. With one long stride, his long arm clamped over the man's mouth. He yanked the unsuspecting man off his feet and against his chest. The blade plunged into his chest, piercing the heart. He held him off the ground until he stopped kicking, then lowered him.

"LT, where are you?" Concern was in the Corporal's voice. Then Weatherman stepped into view and concern grew to fear. His burst cut the man down. He swept the muzzle left to take out the next target, but a shot beat him. The man fell. He assumed it had come from Money but not wanting to risk his life on an assumption, dropped and scurried for cover.

All was silent once more. A slight sound nearby had him turning, ready to engage. Rose slid from the shadows to stand next to him. He stood. She put her lips an inch from his ear. "Clear to the street. There's a jeep waiting for us."

Movement ten yards to their left had both swinging their weapons and taking cover. Someone crashed through the trees to the right in full flight. Money joined them six feet away. He motioned all was clear in his direction. Weatherman hand signaled he was moving and they should cover. Then he crept forward, vanishing in the darkness. He found three bodies. The numbers didn't add up. These three, the one he just shot. The two Money took out and the man running equaled seven. He had only seen six. Were there others hiding in the shadows?

They had to leave this area fast and find their friends.

Something small hit his chest. He ducked and raised his weapon in the direction the projectile had come from. It was too small to be a threat and too close to him to be a distraction. A warning? But if Money and Rose were behind him, who—?

A rifle shot broke the silence and something hit the ground not ten feet away. Weatherman was unusually spooked. He had almost walked right into his death. Someone had saved him. A voice called to him, "I'm coming out, don't shoot."

He recognized the voice, "Give me a word," he said to be sure.

"Weatherman."

That was a good word. "Come." He was sure now his savior was Long Shot.

The man emerged with caution. He waited a second, then said, "Brother, is it good to see you."

"Same. Where's Astronaut?"

"Somewhere around here. He went off with your friend. He's hurt bad. I lured the shooters away from them. If they stayed on course, they're in that direction."

He turned and gave a quick, low whistle. Moments later, Rose came into view from his right and Money emerged from the left. After a quick and joyous reunion, Weatherman said, "Rose, secure the jeep. If Astronaut is hurt, we'll need transport. Money, scout ahead. They'll be coming soon." He and Long Shot set off in search of Astronaut.

They made more noise than they liked but for the moment, felt secure in the fact they were alone. Long Shot risked a call out. "Ellie, it's Long Shot. You out there?"

Nothing. They moved on.

"Any chance they escaped the woods and left the area?"

"Yeah, but that would have taken a heroic effort on her part. Astronaut was out. More like her strength gave out and she hid. The question is whether she left him."

Ten feet further and a shot was fired. The two men dropped as the bullet passed between them and dangerously close. They separated and came at the shooter from two different sides. No other shots came. Weatherman focused on a thicket of vine-like bushes that hung low and covered the ground. He circled around. If Long Shot saw him, he did an excellent job of keeping away. As he crept up behind the thicket, a noise to the right drew the shooter's attention and another bullet. It was all the diversion he needed.

Weatherman bent, snared the legs, and yanked. As the shooter turned to get off a shot at him, he dove on top. The squeal of air and sound forced from the shooter's throat paused his knife from slicing through the tender throat. "Ellie?"

He lifted a bit to see her face. She slapped at him and squirmed, snarling like a wounded animal. He grabbed her face in one hand. "Ellie. Stop. It's me."

He didn't have to say the name. She froze, peered at him, then squealed with joy as she wrapped her arms around his neck and kissed him. He had to break her fierce grip to pull away and keep the tongue from further assault.

"Where's Astronaut?"

"He's right here, and he's hurt. He's unconscious."

She crawled out and Long Shot came out of hiding to assist with lifting Astronaut. They hauled him up between them. "Nice job," Long Shot said to Ellie. They started toward the road.

Chapter Eighteen

Money joined them a minute later. "Got a large party heading our way. At least twenty. Heard multiple vehicles. I think they're working to come up behind us."

Weatherman said, "We need to hurry. Go ahead and let Rose know. Ellie, go with him."

She started to argue but must have thought better of it. She ran to catch Money.

They lifted Astronaut so his feet weren't dragging and increased their pace. By the time they reached the jeep and set him in the back, the sound of engines was approaching fast. Money and Long Shot jumped in back and pinned Astronaut between them. Rose had the engine running and Weatherman sat in the passenger seat. Ellie climbed up and dropped into Weatherman's lap and gave him a wicked smile. Rose drove, keeping the headlights off.

The road curved back toward the base. Ahead was a fork. Rose took the left branch, moving away. Less than a mile later they hit a dead end.

"Is that the expressway we were on?" Rose asked, motioning ahead to the road ten feet above their current position.

"Yes," Weatherman said, having a good idea what was coming next.

"Hold on," he shouted to the back seat as Rose accelerated. Ellie needed no encouragement. She wrapped her arms around Weatherman's neck and pressed closed to him placing her chin on his shoulder.

Rose hit the embankment, and the jeep climbed. The wheels slipped twice but both times caught traction. They reached the top as a convoy of vehicles came into view.

She urged the jeep onward. It crested the top as shots chased them from below.

Rose raced east on the westbound lane until they were next to the minivan. Weatherman lifted and tossed Ellie from his lap, then helped Money and Long Shot lift and carry Astronaut to the van. Rose started to drive but Weatherman called, "Wait." He released Astronaut to the others as they slid him in the back door, then hopped in the jeep's passenger seat. Ellie tried to get in too, but Rose punched the pedal and the jeep shot forward, leaving her behind.

Rose flicked on the headlights to draw any pursuer's eyes toward them. She glanced at Weatherman and smiled.

"Don't say it," he said.

"I think your girlfriend's going to be pissed you abandoned her."

He sighed. "Just drive and try not to get us killed. He turned in his seat to watch behind. Though too dark to be sure, he thought they all made it into the van, including Ellie. Fifty yards past the van the first signs of pursuit showed as headlights shooting upward. A minute later, the headlights leveled, and he knew they had reached the top. They'd be coming after them now. He hoped the others had not been seen or they'd be trapped inside the van.

"Are they up?"

"Yeah, give it a minute to give them a chance to pass the van."

His next look showed two vehicles on the road behind them. They had a good lead and as the road curved north, Rose turned the lights off. Ahead was an exit ramp. Rose shot down it, then turned right, traveling at an unsafe speed. She didn't want to tap the brakes knowing the red lights could be seen a long way.

She sped under the viaduct and along the road to the eastern side of the expressway. Weatherman spotted a road to the right, but it was too open from the expressway. "There," he pointed left.

Rose saw the road that led into a residential area that was surrounded by a large, wooded area. She took the turn at high speed and was forced to drive thirty feet onto a lawn or risk flipping the jeep. She slowed on the soft ground wanting to gain balance and purchase before accelerating again. They drove in front of a house then she aimed the jeep back toward the road. It wound past four houses before they came to a small court.

"Dead end," Rose said. That's okay. Ditch the jeep and we'll lose them on foot."

She drove off the road and buried the jeep in the woods. If they were followed, it would take a thorough search to find the jeep.

They jumped out and ran across the street and into the woods. They weren't thick, which allowed them to move faster, but still offered cover in the dark. They turned south and soon reached the street they had been on. There they dropped to the ground as headlights loomed down the road. Weatherman saw four vehicles, two jeeps and two Humvees stopped on the expressway above them. It was obvious their pursuers didn't know where they had gone. After a brief discussion, one jeep continued down the expressway while the other three vehicles descended the ramp. At the bottom, one Humvee turned east away from them. The remaining jeep and Humvee drove in their direction.

When they reached the street across from them, the jeep turned right. The Humvee continued into the residential street where they had hidden the jeep. Once they were out of view, Weatherman and Rose darted across the street. Through the trees on the right, they could see the jeep making a sweep of the area. They worked their way along a small creek until they were past the jeep. Seconds later, after shining the headlights over the grounds, the jeep drove off to join the Humvee.

It might not take as long as they hoped to find the jeep they hid, so they increased their pace to get as much distance as possible. They reached open ground that had been cleared for overhead electrical wires. They paused for an instant, then sprinted across until they were in the woods again.

"What's the plan?" Rose asked.

"We go back and surveil the van. If it's still there, we settle in and offer cover."

"If it's gone, where would they go?"

"My guess is back to the farmhouse we occupied before we went north."

"Any idea how to get there?"

"Of course."

"Bull shit!"

Weatherman grunted a laugh. "And what would you like me to do, stop at a gas station to ask for directions?"

She laughed. "No."

"Didn't think so."

"You're male. Asking for directions is against your nature."

"I forgot just how unfunny you are."

"You just don't know or appreciate humor."

He was about to make a snappy reply when they noticed lights through the trees to their right. They stopped and ducked.

"Are they coming?" Rose asked.

"No. I think they're on the expressway going back."

"That means they found the jeep."

"Yep." He got up and began moving again. The lights disappeared behind the trees.

"They're not giving up though."

"I doubt it. Most likely going back to get more troops. They'll cordon off an area and begin a search from different directions. We need to determine where that search will commence and ensure we're outside the cordoned area."

"They'll have to guess how far we can go in the time it takes for them to set up the search."

"Yep."

"They don't know what we're capable of."

"No, but I think they're getting the idea. If they have the access, as I think they do, they may already have our files. Whatever they think is normal, they'll expand the search area considering our skill level."

"That means we have to push harder."

"First, we have to see if the van is still there."

"That's going to slow our progress."

"Yep, but we don't have a choice." He angled right toward the expressway.

Chapter Nineteen

They reached the slope up to the expressway and crawled to the top. After scanning the area and seeing no movement, they climbed to the roadway and moved from vehicle to vehicle, watching the opposite side of the road. When they reached the area where they had left the van, they found it was gone.

"You think they drove off on their own or were captured?" Rose asked.

"I think there would be signs of a battle if they were captured."

"Do we leave not knowing for sure?"

"We have two choices. Go back and see for ourselves or move on to the farmhouse."

"If we leave and find they're not at the farmhouse, we may be signing their death warrants."

"I'm thinking they drove away. Otherwise, we'd see their bodies lying here now. If they're not at the farmhouse, we'll know to come back."

Rose thought about it, then said, "The farmhouse then."

They ran down the slope and went cross country. It took two hours to find Goodenow Road. There they found activity. Twice they spotted headlights blocks away.

"They're doing a block-by-block search," Weatherman said.

"That means they don't know where they are."

"Or that they have the others and are looking for us."

"Why would they come here if they lost us miles north of here?"

Weatherman said, "Good point. Let's get to the farmhouse and go from there."

They opted to go wide and east to come in from the far side and away from the search pattern. That choice soon became apparent was the wrong one as the ground ahead was open for a long way in each direction. Any attempt to approach the property made them easy to see. With the eastern sky beginning to lighten, their options were fading.

Weatherman crouched in the last line of trees and the only cover left and studied what lay ahead. They were in a sparse plot of trees and brush north and east of the farmhouse. Each used binoculars to scan the land.

"I don't see anything. You think we got it wrong?" asked Rose.

"They'd choose someplace we knew if possible. This is the last place we were all together."

"You thinking they were captured?"

"I'm thinking something doesn't feel right."

"That famous Weatherman sixth sense kicking in?"

The corner of his mouth twitched in a smile. "You mean the famous sixth sense that had us walking into the midst of a cocaine harvesting operation in the Columbian jungle?"

"Yeah, that would be the one."

"Yep."

She pointed right as she scanned. "We can work closer. That puts us in direct line with the property, gives us a line of sight down the center of the farmhouse grounds, and leaves us only a hundred yards short."

"Uh-huh!" he grunted absently.

After a moment of silence, Rose asked, "What's bothering you?"

"A few things. If they were free, they'd know to come here."

"Okay. I get that. If they were free."

"It's too quiet."

"Meaning?"

"They would hide the vehicle, secure the premises, and work on Astronaut. However, Money is smart enough to know to leave a sign to show they were here." He pointed toward the farmhouse. "He'd post someone on the second floor as the place with the highest and best overall vantage point. Somewhere on the grounds, he'd have something that told us specifically that it was safe to approach. Something that blended in and might not draw a casual observer's attention."

"Like the red flags on the road."

"Yeah, but that was to announce danger or trouble and to get our attention. This would be more subtle. I see nothing."

"Maybe we need a different vantage point."

"Maybe," but his tone suggested he wasn't sure if that mattered. "Okay, let's move. Be aware, however, that where you want to go is the best and closest spot to stage and wait to spring a trap."

They moved deeper into the sparse cover and went west two hundred yards before taking a southern leg. There they slowed and advanced with total stealth. They stopped behind a small pond and settled into the foliage. Again, they did a scan, this time able to see the center and length of the farmhouse property. It had the look and feel of being deserted.

"What now?" asked Rose.

"Keep focused on the farm. I'm going to move a little more west toward the next property. There's a farmhouse over there too."

Rose didn't reply. Weatherman melded with the trees and vanished in silence. It was getting too light for the darkness to offer any camouflage, so Weatherman took his time and blended into whatever the surroundings offered. The brown and green of the environment was something he could make work. Soon, he came to a paved road. There, he crouched and burrowed in, then settled for a good five minutes before raising his head in slow increments to survey the land on the opposite side.

Though the same as his side of the road, he noticed two houses. One was to his right and set back from the road. The other was a larger farmhouse and was completely in the open. A thicker patch of trees and undergrowth surrounded the back of the property, and beyond that he knew was open farmland.

As he studied the two houses, he looked for subtle changes. The blacktop driveway leading to the second house was on the near side and in view. Also in sight were the tracks of compressed grass caused by heavy vehicles leading past the driveway and behind the house.

The house on the left did not offer immediate cover. Any vehicles there had to be well back beyond the house to be hidden. However, whoever occupied the house could not keep from moving the curtains to peer outside.

In the brief time they had stayed at the farmhouse across from these two houses, he had not seen any signs of life. This was clearly a trap. That told him they knew quite a bit about them and may have captured his friends. As he continued to watch, hoping to get an idea of numbers, he gave thought to the possibilities. One, his friends were captured and held hostage. Purpose, information. Two, they had found and killed his friends. He knew unless taken by surprise or overwhelmed, they were not the sort to give up without a fight. Result, death—time to move on. Three, they had discovered the trap and fled, perhaps pursued, most likely not. If those lying in wait had given chase, they would not be here. Question, where would they retreat to?

Weatherman waited another hour but didn't gain much more knowledge for his time. He backed cautiously away and rejoined Rose.

"They're waiting for us," he said.

"Yep. They're at the farmhouse too. A short time ago, your girlfriend managed to escape. However, she didn't have the skill to avoid detection and was recaptured before she got off the property. Three soldiers came from the two barns and corralled her. She kicked and clawed, but she was no match. I give her credit. She's feisty."

She rolled on her side and looked at him. Weatherman knew she was waiting for a directive. "There're only two choices." Rose was smart and experienced. He didn't have to spell them out.

"You know my vote."

He did. It was the same as his. Leaving his friends, his longtime comrades was not an option. They would initiate a rescue despite the odds. However, that didn't mean they had to die making the effort. First order of business was to establish what they were up against. Once they had an idea of numbers, it was time to lessen them. That was going to be a long, slow, and deadly process. No time like the present to get started.

He rolled to his back, closed his eyes, and called up images from the three sites. Within ten minutes, he had worked through a multitude of options and had the best one ready to present. She wasn't going to like it. Not one bit. That made him smile.

Rose had been watching him. When she saw the smile she said, "You bastard."

Chapter Twenty

Stripped down to her bra and with her ACU pants rolled up exposing her legs, a disheveled Rose staggered weakly down the road to the north of the house that was set back. To Weatherman's best calculation, eight enemy combatants were housed there with two out on watch each shift.

Rose sang softly to herself as she went, the sound purposeful to draw attention. Before she came into view from the house, a soldier emerged from the woods, snagged her arm, and dragged her into the woods. Whatever his intention was would forever remain unknown, for as soon as she was hidden from the house, she drove her combat knife through his throat, then ripped it open. She shoved him away to prevent blood spatter.

When she was clear and began redressing, Weatherman, who had been watching in case things got out of control, crept up on the second guard, cupped a large hand over the man's mouth, hauled him backward, and plunged his knife repeatedly through his heart until the man offered no resistance. He set him down and melded back into the foliage.

There he waited patiently for the change of guard. They had clocked the change at every two hours and timed their assault to take out four at once. When the two new guards came out, they called to their comrades. Weatherman was unaware of how Rose drew her opponent in, but he squatted behind a tree and grunted a few times as if struggling to drop a deuce. The man turned his back to give him privacy and Weatherman added him to the collection of bodies.

He watched the house for any unusual activity. By the time Rose joined him, he was sure their attacks had been undetected. The next part of the first plan was bolder. They were going to enter the house as if just getting off guard duty. They had both been in enough camps and bivouacs over their military careers to know what soldiers did in their downtime. Eat, sleep, drink, clean weapons, or play cards. At this early hour, they anticipated finding at least two in the rack. The goal was to avoid a gunfight if possible.

They came to the ranch-style house from an angle to be hidden for as long as possible. Once at the house, they stayed close with their heads down. They entered through the rear door into the kitchen where two men were busy eating MREs. By the time they looked up, Weatherman and Rose were on them. Though they made more noise than intended, a brief struggle resulted in a cry of pain and an upended chair, and the men were dispatched and laid on the floor.

They crouched and waited for anyone to come and check on the noise, but after two minutes with no further sound of movement, they crept down the hall toward the bedrooms. The four doors down the hall were closed. Weatherman motioned he was going left. He didn't have to do more. Rose understood her part.

Weatherman cracked the first door and found a bathroom. It was unoccupied. He did not attempt to close it in case it made a noise and moved on. To the right, he was aware Rose had gone into her first room. Loud snoring came from his second room. He turned the knob slowly and pushed enough to get a glimpse into the room. With the door open, the snores were louder. They covered the creaking of the floorboards as he approached. He stayed low, knowing shadows could penetrate closed eyelids.

As he reached the bed, the man became aware of his presence but by the time his eyes fluttered open and he recognized the danger, his life was already ebbing. He exited and found Rose cracking the last door. He was sure of eight bodies in the house and eight had been dealt with. If there was a ninth or tenth, they were in this room.

Weatherman drew his sidearm and aimed over her head as a backup to her. He would never assume to take the lead from her. She had proven to be an extremely skilled hunter and killer. She cracked the door and had it ripped from her hand. The man raised a gun to shoot her and Weatherman was forced to fire. The bullet tore through the man's forehead and he dropped hard to the floor. Before the body hit, they were moving. Weatherman grabbed the sidearms and spare mags from both men in the kitchen and then caught up to Rose outside the house, moving away from the second house. They were long gone before anyone came in pursuit.

They ran north, staying in the sparse woods. They ran past three other houses and two ponds before coming to the last house. Beyond that, the woods got denser and offered more protection.

"The house or the woods?" Rose asked.

"Don't want to get caught in the house with no way out. Best to keep moving."

"I was thinking more like an ambush to knock the numbers down."

"Good idea, but let's do it from the woods behind the house so we don't have to escape over open ground."

With a plan in mind, they raced around the house and put it to their backs. Once inside the cover of the trees, they separated and found a blind to set up in. Then the wait began. It was a tossup as to whether killing more enemies or getting more distance was the greater need. To Weatherman's mind, they would be pursued regardless of what they did. It was best to make them pay for their efforts.

Almost ten minutes later, with still no pursuit in sight, Weatherman was about to signal to fall back when the sound of an engine reached him. A jeep with three men in it, two in the seats and one behind the mounted fifty caliber machine gun, drove along the road and went left of the house. It moved at a slow speed as the passenger and gunner scanned the woods for a target.

He caught movement as men walked through the woods to the left of the house. A loud crash drew attention to the house. A man came around the side and gazed out at the tree line where they hid. A second man exited the house through the rear door after clearing it. To the right was another road. Four more men moved along it on foot. They were pinned though their pursuers were unaware.

If they took out the two men in front of them, they'd be caught in a pincer with only one direction to go, straight north. They had no idea where the woods ended or what they might run into further along that path. For the moment, they waited.

The two men had a brief discussion, then one motioned with his chin toward the woods and they set off coming right at Rose. He had no opportunity to adjust his position to get closer. Any movement at this point would easily be seen. He waited, sliding both knife and handgun out and pushing the slung rifle to his back. With sloth-like movements, he slid one knee up to have it underneath him for a push off. To cover the distance needed to help Rose, his first move had to be explosive.

From their path, it looked as if the two men would enter the trees less than two yards from Rose's position. That left them twenty yards from him. He got to all fours as he passed to their periphery, then to a crouch. He pictured the scene. Rose would be making her move any second. He needed to help her but at this distance, the best he could do was serve as a distraction. He reached up and shook a branch. Both men whirled in his direction, guns ready to fire.

Weatherman had to wait for Rose before moving, or he'd be mowed down before he got two steps. One man arched back and cried out. He moved. He now had a visual of the second man turning toward his partner. Though Rose had already punctured the man with her knife, she held him up to serve as a shield.

The second moved to get a shot. Weatherman had no chance of reaching him in time to use the knife. As the man angled to her side, Weatherman raised the gun, stopped, and fired a quick three rounds that staggered the man. Two rounds hit but from the side and did not put him down. As he turned toward Weatherman to fire, Rose pitched the dead man into him, knocking the burst offline, and then pounced on him. Three quick, deep thrusts, and the man was down.

They had no time to strip the bodies nor any way to carry the extra loads. Weatherman signaled to move right where the fewer enemy was, and Rose fell in stride next to him.

"Four men all on foot. They'll be coming. We need to take them before those from the left converge."

He stepped away, found a toppled tree with a large trunk, and knelt, swinging his AR up. Rose went five yards further and broke to the left, dropping under the thick drooping branches of a Blue Spruce. The trunk would not offer protection being rather slender, but the initial cover was complete.

It didn't take long for the untrained soldiers to advance, announcing their exact position from the haste of their movements.

Rose caught sight of a target and triggered first. Though Weatherman could not see the result, he assumed the target was down. Three to go. He had no clear target but as return fire ripped through the Blue Spruce, he zeroed in on a shooter. With only slim glimpses, he made an adjustment and fired. The target went down and he moved.

Rose took down another one and the final member fled for his life.

Weatherman tore past Rose and ran deeper into the woods. He could hear her running somewhere behind him. He wanted distance from the final group to set up for the next attack. He calculated as he ran. Three in the jeep and an unknown amount he placed at six men on foot. If they kept the fifty cal out of the equation, they had a chance to get through this. That was providing reinforcements didn't arrive before they were done.

Speaking of which, how was it possible for them to have so many bodies to throw at them in such an abbreviated time? Was there a base nearby? Michigan was one of the core states listed in the conspiracy, but that still meant transporting troops from hours away. With all the damage the opposition had taken over the past few days, they had to be running low on combatants. Didn't they?

Chapter Twenty-One

They moved with speed, eating up ground in large chunks. The left and right roads closed to a point of only a ten-yard separation. They skirted between and kept to the woods. Weatherman began to think that perhaps setting another ambush might be a mistake. Outrunning and hiding from the small pursuit posse might be smarter. What they needed was wheels to allow them to get to the far side of the farmhouse while everyone was drawn here.

He had the bad feeling that whoever the authorities were, they could throw an unwavering and never-ending supply of troops and equipment at them. The numbers didn't add up. He was missing something.

The jeep's engine was easy to hear as it approached from their left. Through the trees ahead, he could see the ground was open. They were out of room to run. It was time to decide their next move.

Rose called. "Right."

Without thought or question, he angled right. In that direction was a road followed by a long driveway into a parking lot. Across the road, the woods and undergrowth continued. They darted across the open ground and reached cover without drawing fire. After a short while, they began angling north again. With no signs or sounds of pursuit close, they settled into a steady pace. They followed the direction the trees went until they reached a paved road. There they stopped and did an area scan. They didn't hear anyone in the woods and the jeep engine could no longer be heard.

They crossed the road. Fifty yards later, they came to the back of a house. Around the front, they found a car and a pickup in the driveway.

"Check the house," Weatherman said. "See if you can locate a key for either vehicle."

Rose moved to the door. She tried the knob. It turned and the door opened. She took one step in and recoiled. Weatherman knew what that meant. Bodies. Whoever lived here had died inside the house. Rose sucked in large gulps of air, then held the last one before braving the foul odor.

Weatherman went to the truck and tried the door. It was locked. He pressed a hand to the window, then his face, looking for a key. He moved to the car. It was the same, locked and no key visible.

Rose ran out and released an explosive breath. She sucked air in short gasps as she walked forward and held out a hand. A ring of keys dangled from her fingers. He took the keys and found they belonged to the car. He got in and started the engine. Rose came over, slid into the passenger seat, and gave him a nasty look. Between pants, she said, "Next time you go into the house with the corpses."

Weatherman backed down the driveway and then down the street to the east. He ran straight down Bemmes Road for two miles before turning south on Klemme Road. He thought that gave them enough distance to get past the watchers at the farmhouse without being seen. Though they reached Goodenow Road, he realized it only went east but the farmhouse was back to the west. They had to go further south before cutting across. He continued to Brunswick Road, which he calculated would put them a good three miles south of the farmhouse. From there, he slowed to avoid driving into an ambush.

Brunswick ended at Yates. Though Weatherman couldn't remember the name of the road the farmhouse sat on, he was sure it wasn't Yates. He turned south, then went west on Eagle Lake, knowing it brought them closer to their destination. When they hit Park, Rose said, "This is it."

He didn't ask a stupid question like, "are you sure?" If Rose said it was the one, he accepted that as fact. He stopped short of the intersection. He felt as if he had been running all the while they were in the car. His heart rate was still accelerated. The corners held open farmland on three sides, with a house on the fourth. Weatherman crossed Park, drove up the driveway of the house, and around back. He parked and they got out and broke into the house. They needed a rest and a plan.

Unfortunately, they had not taken any of the food or water from the van. They had nothing. A search of the cupboards did turn up a jar of peanut butter and saltine crackers. They munched on that in silence. After a while, Weatherman found it difficult to swallow, then heard a snick and a hiss. He glanced over to see Rose guzzling down a warm diet pop. She stopped, shook the can, eyed him, then took another gulp before handing him the rest. He drank it greedily but saved a gulp so he could have another few crackers before washing down.

With their quick meal finished, they scooted to the front window and watched the road as they discussed options.

"I think the farmhouse is too close to drive," Rose said. "We'll be seen."

"And the ground is open, allowing them to see a long way."

"Our only hope is that their focus is drawn north. "I'm not sure how close we can get, but we can't afford to get caught in the open. Especially if they bring in the fifty cal."

"Not to mention we have no idea how many we're facing."

"Yeah, There's that."

"Don't tell me you don't have a plan. I know you better than that."

"Not a good one."

She laughed. "Are they ever?"

He smiled and they held each other's gaze for an instant before averting.

"Okay, here's my plan, but you're not gonna like it."

"Let me guess. This time I'm completely naked."

He laughed. "No, you can save that for if we survive."

She got serious. "Yeah. If—"

"I'm going to find the best place to snipe from. I'll give you a chance to get closer to the stables. Once I start shooting, you work your way inside and free our friends."

"And then?"

He laughed again. "And then? Hell, we'll both probably be dead before the 'and then.'" His face softened. "No matter what, you get our people as far from here as you can."

"You know you may be a Tier One weenie, but that doesn't make you superman."

"I'm aware."

The look in her eyes said she understood Weatherman did not expect to be joining them. She lowered her eyes as if she had something to say, then blew out a breath and started for the door. She stopped and came back. Her eyes met his then she kissed him lightly on the lips. "In case we don't survive."

"We better. I want more of that."

"Of course, you do. You're male. Killing and sex are all you think about. If you want more, then you best survive." She turned and left.

Weatherman looked out the window, purposely avoiding watching her go. He preferred the kiss to be the last memory of her.

He gave her twenty minutes to make her way west of the farmhouse. She would travel a greater distance, but it would take him longer to move across open land. He checked his mags. Three full and a partial plus what he had in the AR. His goal was to spend them all before they took him down. He also had four full mags for the handgun. He could do damage, but it was limited being in the open. His one advantage was they had to close on him to have a chance of hitting him. They'd pay dearly for that honor.

Weatherman left the house and jogged across the street. He angled away from the road toward a narrow band of grass, brush, and trees. They were spread out over a long distance, but the little cover was better than none. He reached a longer stretch of trees and moved within them until he reached a break. There he squatted and lifted his glasses. The farmhouse was still a good distance away. Activity on the grounds told him something was happening though from where he was, it was difficult to discern what.

He checked his surroundings, then dashed for the next line of cover. When it ended, he was looking at forty yards of ground with nothing to obscure him from whoever might be watching. He took a long time with the glasses studying the second-story windows of the house. If they had positioned a spotter there, he'd be easy to see.

Ahead of him was a dirt path running through the center of the narrow strip. It curved right and moved toward the road. The ground was inches above the crop land. It wasn't much, but it was all he had. He got down on his belly and crawled, moving a foot a minute. An hour later, he reached the place where the path curved. The narrow strip continued straight and now had trees along both sides.

Weatherman got to his feet and jogged in a low crouch needing to make up some time. He didn't want Rose to be stuck in one place for too long. Even an untrained eye might get lucky and discover her.

    To his surprise, he found the eight-foot-wide band of shrubs and the occasional tree running between the fields went all the way to Goodenow Road, which would place him even with the farmhouse. He didn't want to go that far. Rose needed room to maneuver so he stayed south of the property. He settled into a space that allowed a view between Quonset hut and house. The helicopter blocked a portion of the view. He didn't have many targets, and because of the number of buildings on the lot he had a limited angle. He'd have to acquire a target and then move to gain another. However, to get at him they had to cross fifty yards of open ground.

    He studied the scene with confidence. He'd take a substantial number of them down before they closed in to finish him. "Okay, Rosie, it's up to you now."

Chapter Twenty-Two

Rose had jogged west down the road away from the house, knowing she had more distance to cover than Weatherman did. As she ran, her mind sifted through viable options and alternate endings. She refused to allow Weatherman to give up his life to save the others. Somehow, she would complete her rescue mission and then save Weatherman. He was not dying today.

She went past the next road and midway down the block before running through a field of what looked to be corn. This early in the year, the growth was but a leafy sprout. Though moving over mostly open ground, she had gone far enough that anyone watching would miss her unless they had binoculars trained in her direction. Ten minutes later, she had covered the entire distance needed to be level with the farmhouse just a half a mile to the west. With the sun up, she was easier to see but also had a good view in all directions should any vehicles be spotted.

Rose advanced at a crouched jog. Ahead of her and across Goodenow Road was a stretch of buildings belonging to the farm one down from theirs. The buildings ran north and south which gave her the cover she needed to arrive safely and unseen. She pressed against the wall for a quick rest. Then worked to the end of a long metal barn. There she was able to have a full view of the farmhouse where her comrades were being held.

To reach the farm, Rose had to traverse a hundred yards of open ground with no spots of cover along her path. She studied the approach for a long time. Once Weatherman began his diversion, it would draw people away from the buildings but also make them alert. She decided she needed to be on the move before the shooting began and approach from the northern side of the road. A spaced line of small trees ran along the road that offered cover. Past that was a small house that sat kitty-corner to the farmhouse. From there, coming at an angle, she only had forty yards to go to reach the first building, though it was across open ground and the intersection. Still, forty yards was better than a hundred.

She moved to the opposite end of the house. Then after checking the road, she darted forward. From the north came a jeep. She heard it before she saw it and was already on the ground when it passed. The jeep went down to the farmhouse driveway and turned in. She did not see who was inside. Since no brake lights flashed on, she assumed she had not been seen. Before she could move again, the distant echo of gunshots reached her. Weatherman had begun.

He estimated he was looking at a two-hundred-yard shot, which was not exceptionally long. He had trained and accomplished longer. However, that was with a sniper rifle specifically set to his specs. This weapon, though capable of reaching that distance was untested and lacked the overall power. Still, his main purpose was to draw them to him, allowing Rose to rescue the others. Once they got closer, he'd worry about his kill count.

He first created his blind to ensure his footprint was as limited and small as possible. He tore branches and draped them over his weapon and body. Once confident it would take several shots before he was located, he made adjustments to the sights, assessed for wind, and began controlling his breathing. When he was ready, he settled in, made a minor adjustment to the sight, and searched for his first target. He didn't have long to wait.

A jeep drove down the road coming from the north and turned into the driveway. It was not the same one that had chased them earlier. This one had two people inside and no fifty cal. The driver parked next to the helo. The passenger got out and lifted a heavy toolbox from the back, then disappeared behind the helo. Weatherman assumed he was a mechanic but when he last was here, both helos were working. That suggested something else. He had been so focused on his targets that he just realized one of the birds was gone. Had these people taken it, or had Long Shot and Astronaut hidden it at another location? Didn't matter. He had a job to do.

The driver checked on the mechanic, then came back to the jeep. He lifted a foot to slide in and Weatherman fired. The shot dropped more than expected, telling him the weapon lacked power. He had sighted on the upper back wanting a large target until he knew the AR's capabilities. The shot struck the lower back a good six inches down.

The man arched back, and his hands clutched at the wound. Though damaged, he was not dead. Still, Weatherman was confident he was out of the fight. The echo of the shot washed across the grounds. He caught glimpses of movement but did not have a shot. He waited patiently. They would only have a vague idea of his location until he fired again.

The mechanic crawled to the jeep and stayed there. Another man came from around the Quonset hut and said something to the mechanic. He stupidly advanced closer as he talked, obviously unaware of the shooter's location. Weatherman made sure it was the last stupid thing he did. Having adjusted his aim, the bullet hit the man in the abdomen. He staggered back before his legs gave out and he dropped to his butt, stunned to see his blood leaking from his body.

Weatherman ignored him and scanned for the next target. The more experienced men would have a general idea as to his position. If so, they weren't spreading the word fast enough. Two men ran toward the Quonset hut carrying rifles. Weatherman had time to drop one as his target ran into the shot. He took another running step and then collapsed. The second man stumbled and fell behind the hut and out of Weatherman's line of sight.

He was surprised to see the lack of response. Perhaps whoever was in charge was as clueless as his men. With no one currently tracking him, Weatherman slid back and crawled twenty yards to the south before setting up again. By the time he was ready to engage again, he had lots of targets and they were all coming his way.

In rapid succession, he targeted, triggered, and dropped three men. Shots were being aimed in his direction but not close enough to matter. Most still had no idea of his location. That was what happened when you took anyone into your militia and didn't have the time or ability to train them properly. He moved again. This time he set up faster.

A dozen men had taken up positions around the buildings closest to him and were sniping back. Two jeeps shot across the grounds before he was reset and turned north on the road moving away from him. He'd be seeing them soon coming from his flank.

No one attempted to get closer. Someone had produced a plan. Keep him occupied and pinned down until the flanking squad could engage. Regardless, they'd still have to cross the fields to get to him even if they came cross country in the jeeps. He exchanged shots with the men hoping Rose had time to reach her destination.

He fired twice more, then retreated again, this time back to where the path curved. This allowed him to work to a more straight on shot deep into the grounds in front of the house. He didn't have any targets, but that didn't matter if the enemy remained focused on him. He spotted the jeep barreling over the soft, uneven ground of the field to his left. The second jeep must be working around him to cut him off.

He targeted the driver, who sat low in his seat. The others were hunkered down below the dash and not a target. He fired into the windshield, hoping to get a reaction from the driver. It came as he braked on reflex, throwing those in the back forward. One man appeared between the two front seats and Weatherman buried a round in his face. The jeep swerved away then. The second man in the back seat climbed out over the back and burrowed into the ground.

Weatherman risked a peek behind him and located the second jeep coming up behind him. They'd soon have him in a three-sided crossfire. He couldn't allow that to happen. He fired once at the man on the ground, twice at the farm buildings, then moved to the opposite side of the path facing back the way he came.

The second jeep opted not to take the cross-country route. Instead, it drove down the street and stopped a hundred yards back to allow its three passengers to get out. The driver then swung the wheel around and drove away at high speed. As the three men broke for the limited cover along the road, Weatherman fired and hit one. The other two dove for the ground as Weatherman exchanged magazines.

He had two shooters behind him, one to the west and a dozen or so to the north. The two men behind him worked their way into a narrow row of trees and brush like his own cover. They were a hundred yards behind him. Weatherman glanced at a house near the road equal distance between him and the two men. Though restricted, the house offered substantial cover. He'd never get back out again, but he'd last longer. If Rose got the others out, it would be worth it. In the open with shooters all around, he wasn't going to last long.

Decision made, he ran along the path until even with the house. He broke from cover and sprinted toward the side of the house. The shooters behind him had a long, albeit open shot at him. The two men now in front of him had no shots with the house in their path. The man to the west had a shot but had to get up on one knee to take it and was not a good shot. He had no idea how to judge and lead a moving target.

Weatherman made it to the house without significant danger. Two shots careened off the brick side of the house four feet away. They had to come from the farmhouse shooters. He worked around to the front and up the small stairs to the front door. He crashed into and through the wooden door numbing his shoulder. It was a stupid move. He should have kicked it in. It would have saved the abuse to his body.

The door cracked and flung inward. Weatherman fell through the doorway, then rolled to his feet and was a blur of action. He kicked the door closed and then dragged the sofa over, pushing it against the door to hold it in place. The room wasn't big. It was a family room with a kitchen with a space to eat in just behind. A small island divided the kitchen and dining area. That gave him good cover should they get inside.

He quickly flipped the kitchen table and set it next to the island. He checked the rear window. The two men behind him were maneuvering to get a shooting position on the house. The shooter to the west had been joined by the two other surviving members in the jeep who teamed up with the other two. Five across the back. He let them settle in fifty yards behind the house and hurried to the front.

Down the road, a group of men sprinted toward the house, perhaps hoping their blinding speed was enough not to get shot. Weatherman kicked the sofa to one side, opened the door, and stepped out onto the porch. He sighted and triggered the entire magazine down the street, sending three men to the ground with assorted wounds. They picked up additional damage when striking the blacktop roadway at high speed. Others suffered minor injuries while trying to dive out of the way of the barrage.

    The battle was engaged and the siege was about to commence. He hoped the opening salvo was enough to allow Rose to reach the farmhouse.

Chapter Twenty-Three

Rose wanted to close the distance, so crawled from one tree to the next. She didn't bother going to the house but kept going along the road. That cut fifteen yards off the distance she needed to cross. She lay in the tall grass and watched as men and vehicles raced down the road to where Weatherman was shooting. Rose was surprised at the number of soldiers hidden on the property. With all of them gone, how many were still in the barn? They wouldn't leave the prisoners unguarded.

She gave a long look around the property, stopping on a man in a suit and a woman in a skirt and blouse. They were staring down the road in the direction of the gunfight. Had they arrived in the jeep? Another man walked into view. He wore a uniform that identified him as an officer, although from that distance Rose had no idea what rank. Over the last few days, she'd had her fill of pseudo-officers.

They turned and walked toward the house. Once they were out of sight, Rose ran across the road and to the rear of the first stable. The back door had been closed, leaving the top half of the split door open. She peered inside. A Humvee was parked inside but no one was with it. She moved on.

She noticed the chicken coop was empty. The group who had tried to steal the hens must have taken them. At the gap between the two stables, she paused and then stepped across. Both sections of the door here were closed. A small space existed between the two halves that allowed her to see inside. At the far end were two armed guards standing in the doorway. On the floor, tied to the posts that made up the horse stalls were her friends.

Money and Long Shot were making signals and mouthing silent words. They were plotting something. Ellie watched the guards, standing her own watch for Money and Long Shot. Astronaut, though sitting up, still looked in bad shape. She guessed he had a concussion. He was not involved in the planning.

Rose watched for a minute. She had to take out the guards in silence for an escape to have any hope of success. That meant knife work which meant up close and personal. That wasn't easy to do with two guards. Her best option might be to force them inside at the barrel of her gun.

Back at the gap between the buildings, she pushed her AR forward and walked the three-foot-wide space with caution to avoid bumping into either sidewall. She reached the end, took a deep breath, and stepped out, weapon leveled. She caught one guard with his back to her. He was looking inside the stables. The second guard was not in sight. *Inside or had he left? Damn!* She could have taken this one with a knife.

She rammed the barrel into his back, shoving him forward. He let out an exclamation of pain and arched back. She ripped the rifle from his shoulder and pushed with her barrel. "Inside now, or I blow a hole in your back." He moved as he fumbled for his gun. The other man was inside, bending over Ellie. He was undoing her blouse. She had a wicked smile on her face. Had she lured him in?

At the guard's cry of pain, the man inside turned to look. Rose lifted the rifle as her captive fumbled for his handgun and drove it down on the back of his head. He was taller, and the angle wasn't conducive for a rendering strike. He dropped to one knee, still conscious.

The second guard raised his rifle to shoot Rose, but Ellie lashed out with a foot and kicked the man in the side of his knee, buckling the leg. Rose hit the downed guard with a staggering blow that split his scalp, then leveled the rifle at the second guard before he could bring his gun on target.

"You won't shoot," he said. "Everyone will know you're here. You'll be dead in seconds."

"I will shoot and no one will hear. They're all down the street tending to other matters. Besides, you'll never know the outcome because you'll be dead. Set the rifle down." She moved toward the others. With one hand on the trigger, she slid her knife from its sheath and squatted between Money and Ellie. Rose smiled at the man knowing if he was going to make a move, it would happen now. Her smile was to tell him she hoped he did.

The look froze him, unsure of its meaning. She lowered the knife but could not see where she needed to slice. A glance down was all the guard needed to get off a shot. He still hadn't lowered his gun. Rose jabbed the knife into the post, edge down, then stood.

Ellie looked at the knife, then at Rose, puzzled.

"You're a smart lady. Figure it out."

Money told her what to do. She raised her hands and began sawing back and forth under the blade until the rope parted. Rose heard her grunt as she worked the knife from the post. That brought a second smile to her lips.

"If you're still holding that gun by the time they're all free, you'll force me to kill you. Set it down and allow yourself to be tied up and you will live."

"Nah, you'll kill me."

"I'll kill you for sure if you don't set it down. Besides, I could have killed your friend there but only knocked him out."

The man risked a peek. "Looks like you killed him."

"It's a head wound. They bleed a lot. He won't die."

Behind her she heard Money stand. Rose watched the guard. He thought he was being slick. Every few seconds he inched his barrel toward her. "Don't do that. This isn't worth dying for."

He whipped the gun toward her and she fired. The bullet plowed through his chest. He got off a shot, but it was too early. He looked down at the red blossom forming on his chest. Surprise registered. He looked at her.

"Don't give me that look. I did warn you." She walked closer and pulled the gun from his weakened grip. She slid the handgun out and tossed it back. The guard blinked a few times and began to tip to the side. He lay on the ground blinking, then his eyes fixed.

Ellie freed Long Shot then Money said, "Ellie, go open the rear door."

Rose glanced back and saw her run to do so. Money moved to free Astronaut when the front of the stable filled with armed men. A woman in a skirt and blouse stood behind them. "I suggest you drop your weapons or this stable will be filled with your blood."

Rose sneaked a look at Money. Though he held the handgun she had taken from the guard, Long Shot was empty-handed. They had two guns against six, all ARs. She sighed and bent to put her weapons down. As she did, she realized Ellie was gone. Had the woman run off? For an instant, the thought angered her, but she let it go. Why should she stay? She had a chance to get away. *Go, Ellie. Be free—be safe—be a long way from here.*

The woman in the skirt and blouse entered with the suit following a step behind. She had a wicked, evil smile. She stopped short of Rose and eyed her. Rose read her immediately. She liked power, liked to be in control. She had authority and used it.

"You must be the one they call Blood Rose." The woman circled her, eyeing her up and down.

Though Rose remained impassive, inside something stirred, something close to fear. This woman was danger and death. She was a different sort of killer than Rose was, but a killer nonetheless.

"Yes, this one will do nicely. It's not often I get to interrogate a woman capable of withstanding my, ah, techniques. You'll be an interesting challenge. I hope you are as tough as your file says you are."

File?

"We'll start with her. Take her to the other stable. I'll work on her there."

The woman pivoted and marched out of the stable. Rose watched her go, stunned at what might face her over the next few hours. True, her advanced training had prepared her for this moment, but training was one thing, reality another. She did make one vow, though, as two guards grabbed her roughly and shoved her forward. No matter what this woman did to her, Rose was going to kill her.

Weatherman stepped back inside and changed magazines. He was already down to two full and one partial. They would take time to organize. He had time to fortify the house. If possible, he wanted to keep them focused on this one section of the house. That meant he had to prevent or slow them from entering the bedrooms. That wasn't likely, but he could keep them from entering the family room.

He worked as fast as he could, dragging dressers from the bedrooms and down the hallway. He used one to block the end of the hall and then set the others along the front and back of the kitchen and family room for additional cover. Then he set nightstands in the hall. Next, he yanked mattresses and box springs off the three beds and set them in the hallway. They were awkward to handle and would not stop bullets. While the intruders worked to get past them, they were easy targets.

Lastly, he grabbed every article of clothing in all three closets and piled them in the hall. They weren't much of an impediment other than they might tangle around legs and slow advances. At any rate, he'd know when they were in the house.

After checking the windows in the front and rear and seeing no movement yet, he worked the refrigerator to the rear door. They could still get in, but it would take a concerted effort, and once through, they'd be in no position to shoot or defend.

He had three protective zones and had done all he could. It was up to Rose now. He settled in at the front window where most of the attackers were positioned. He watched and waited for them to make the first move.

Chapter Twenty-Four

The attack began fifteen minutes later when a jeep pulled up to the periphery of the scene. Though Weatherman did not recognize the man, he did know an officer when he saw one and this one looked to be high ranking judging from the adornments on his chest and collar. *Was he a general? Was he even real military?* Whatever he was, he at least had a military bearing.

The assault commenced with an all-out barrage. Weatherman wondered if they had an unending supply of bullets. The windows shattered, glass imploded, and shards flew. He had anticipated that and had used a wooden TV dinner tray as a shield. His hands took nicks, but otherwise the glass had no ill effect on him.

The bullets punched into the interior walls. He didn't fear penetration from the outside as the walls were brick. The onslaught shredded pictures and knick-knacks. He waited patiently for the first assault to end before peering through the bottom of the curtain.

Instructions had been given for the second wave of shooting to cover the advance of four men to the side of the house. Weatherman stationed to the side of the window and managed to cut down two of the invaders before they reached safety. They would attempt to enter through the bedroom windows. They would die trying to get down the hall.

He crawled to the back and noticed only four men there. One of them had joined the other two on the side of the house. He noticed one of the shooters in the back was getting bold. Instead of staying low and behind cover when he fired, he popped up to shoot and then dropped back. It was a very untrained approach. Weatherman again wondered as to the professionalism of this new militia. But given the choice of dying or fighting, you got what you asked for—amateurs. That meant they were much more likely to make mistakes as this man was doing and to break under pressure.

Weatherman lined up the shot, keeping well back from the window. When the man popped up again, he didn't even get off the shot. He flopped back and never popped up again.

He heard the crack of glass in the bedroom. They'd be afraid at first, but when nothing happened, they'd become emboldened and come in. He'd let them for the main reason of taking their weapons and ammo. Before they entered, he slid to the front and checked the window looking to get an angle on the so-called general. He was still there standing on the far side of the jeep with a radio to his head. Weatherman took his time. He didn't have a large target to hit, but then he didn't need much.

It was a headshot. He steadied as a fresh barrage of shots came from the front. He was sure they didn't know he was there, so must have been to cover the entry of the three men on the side of the house. He ignored the distraction, focused, and broke the trigger. The officer began sitting in the jeep as the shot was fired. His hands went up to grab the windshield to guide his bulk into the seat. The altered position doomed the shot, but the bullet struck the radio which was over his head and tore it and a finger from his hand. The man clutched his hand and rolled out of the jeep.

Weatherman swore in anger at the miss but could hear the man wail. It was small satisfaction. He watched as the driver slid low in the seat and began to move, allowing the general to crawl alongside out of the line of fire.

Outside, the shooting stopped, stunned by the shrieks of their leader. Inside, Weatherman heard the bedroom door creak. They were coming. He crawled beneath the window to the wall next to the hallway and waited. They were struggling to walk his obstacle course. He pictured the scene. One would advance while a second tried to control the mattresses and box springs. The third would be covering them, standing in the doorway of the bedroom with his weapon aimed down the hall. He wouldn't have a good shot with his comrade in the way, but he had to go first.

Weatherman knelt, readied his mental and physical moves, then pivoted to face down the hall. The first man had his head down trying to navigate the obstacles. He was a third of the way down the hall and held a handgun. The second man was crouched, holding a mattress and box spring straight up. His head was up, but his hands were occupied. The third man, as expected, had a rifle aimed down the hall. However, he was across the hall from Weatherman. To get off a shot, he had to shoot past his comrades. He hesitated, fearing he'd hit his own team. Weatherman had no such concerns. He acquired his target and went fully automatic, hosing them all down, starting from back to front.

Outside, the shooting had stopped as they waited for a sign the sneak attack had worked.

Someone shouted, "What are you waiting for? Go. Go. Go."

Weatherman smiled. An officer showing his bravery by sending good men to their deaths. He changed magazines and moved to the front window. Six men were sprinting toward the house. He wanted to conserve ammo, so instead of using the entire mag, he snapped two shots at each, hitting the first two and wounding the next two as they dove for the ground. The last two managed to scamper back to safety as the remaining men gave covering fire. He could easily have finished the two wounded men, but there was no point. Their deaths were a waste of life, and they were no longer threats. Besides, he didn't want to use the bullets.

With the scene unthreatening for the moment, he went into the hallway, stripped the bodies of weapons and ammo, and found two canteens with water, a small snack pack of almonds, and a protein bar. The handguns had assorted calibers, but the ARs the men used were a match.

As he patrolled the house from back to front, he thumbed rounds into mags. When the loose rounds were all to capacity, he unloaded partial mags and filled others. When done, he was back to four full spares and a partial, plus the one in the rifle. He changed that one out for a full one, then married the two partials. He set the handguns around the room not wanting the bulk of them carried, but pocketed the two extra magazines that fit his handgun.

It would be a waiting game now. The question was what other assets they had available to send against him. His thoughts drifted to Rose. Had she been successful? Were they free?

He drank a little of the water, swishing it around his mouth first, and fought off the urge to close his eyes as the adrenaline ebbed from his veins. Weatherman ate the protein bar as he moved to the back window. The three surviving shooters there had separated to get different shooting lines. If he was still alive by nightfall, he planned to take them out and escape out the back. That was his only option.

A shot was fired, and a bullet impacted the wall inches in front of his face. Weatherman dropped and crawled quickly to the front corner. He peered out and found someone had moved a Humvee onto the farmland fifty yards out. A man lay on top with a scoped rifle. It was not a sniper's rifle but had the power and accuracy to be deadly. The shooter was not highly skilled, or Weatherman would be dead, but he was good enough to be a threat. The higher elevation gave him a good vantage point into the house, limiting Weatherman's ability to cover back and front without taking precautions. That slowed his reaction time to fend off an assault.

He was surprised they hadn't thought about it sooner. His other fear had been that they'd bring in the fifty-caliber machine gun he saw on the jeep. Those rounds would chew through anything he had available to use as cover. His options were fading.

Weatherman dropped to the floor and moved to the barrier in front of the hallway. He scooted the furniture to the side and crawled down the hall, hurrying to the last bedroom on the right. After cracking the door open and peering inside, he entered and moved to the small window in the front of the house. He ducked underneath and rose at the corner. He had a line of sight at the Humvee. The sniper was slightly elevated over him limiting his target, but he did have one. Even a wound changed the threat. If this man was their best shooter, which made sense, then taking him out in any capacity hindered the potential. The man was as much a weapon as the rifle he used. It would give others pause about taking his place.

Weatherman stood back, took the cord from the blinds, and wrapped it around the barrel to steady his shot. The jagged glass still in the frame was not a deterrent. He sighted just behind the scope where he had a view of the side of the shooter's head. It was not a long shot. He eased back on the trigger and sent the round. The bullet hit the rear of the scope and deflected. Though it still struck the shooter, it was not a kill shot. The man rolled, clutching the side of his head. His hands were coated with blood. He fell off the Humvee.

Silence ensued as shock and surprise gripped the soldiers, then shots were directed at the bedroom window. By then, Weatherman was already in the hall. Before he left, he used his knife to sever the cord. With the bedroom door closed. He tied the cord securely around the knob, then stretched it to the bedroom door across the hall. He tied off that end. Though it wouldn't hold anyone out for long, it would slow them down and give him a chance to react.

    He regained the front room and checked both sides. No one moved and the shooting died down. He had a respite for a time. He moved to the rear window and set up with his aim on the last man in the line of three. He was a tier-one operative and, as such, was a skilled marksman. He settled in with a sniper's mentality. The man would make a mistake and show too much of himself. It would cost him his life.

Chapter Twenty-Five

An hour passed and was chased by a second. Did those in charge hope to wear him down? Time was his ally, not theirs. In the first ten minutes of the third hour, the man he had targeted made his mistake. Perhaps he thought to change locations. Maybe he had to pee—whatever the reason, it was his last act. The bullet ripped through the side of his head, and now he had two to deal with when he made his escape.

Though the shot stirred those in front, no one knew what happened, so no response came. He rewarded his patience and skill by eating the almonds and taking another short drink of water. Then he slid to the other side of the window and eyed the two remaining men. Who would break first? They both looked nervous. He didn't want to set up on one of them yet preferring to give his eyes a rest from the constant strain. There was still time.

Midday had arrived. He still had a good seven to eight hours of daylight left. He tried to put himself in the mind of whoever was in charge but quickly gave up. If he had been in charge, this standoff would be over already and he'd be dead. The lack of leadership was encouraging. The longer it took for them to form a plan of attack, the better for him and for Rose.

From out front, a voice called to him. That surprised him. Someone should've done so long ago. It just reemphasized the lack of true military leadership running this so-called militia. He was curious to see where this discussion led.

"You in the house. I'm guessing you're Weatherman."

The fact the man knew his name surprised him. Then a bad thought came to him. Did one of his team break?

"I have a friend of yours out here who would love to see you again. You might say her life depends on it."

The blood froze in his veins. Without looking, he knew they had Rose. With reluctance, he moved to the front window. He hesitated, not wanting to verify his thought. When he did look, his heart caught in his throat. They had Rose. If they had her, the rescue operation had failed.

Her hands were bound behind her and she could barely stand. Her face had been battered. Her right eye was swollen shut and the left was halfway there. Blood seeped from wounds all over her arms and legs. Someone had taken a knife to the sides of her face.

Two men held her up. The general, now with a bandaged hand, held a handgun to the side of Rose's head. She looked unaware of her situation. Her lips moved. He stepped back and used the scope. Her split lips were difficult to read, but she repeated the same two words over and over. He didn't have to read her lips to know what she said. *Kill me!*

His heart sank. He knew what she wanted. Knew if he was in her situation he'd ask for the same. She did not want to be used against him and was willing to die to prevent him from being taken. He knew in his heart it was what she wanted and was also the right thing to do. She was dead no matter what. He was the only one left to avenge her sacrifice. He would not sell his life cheaply.

He looked around hoping for a way out. The general wasn't taking any chances. He had brought out more men. In the field across from the house was a line of vehicles. Three Humvees bracketed two jeeps with fifty cals. They had brought out the big guns for him. One way or the other the general planned to end this. The question was why? Why use Rose at all? Why not just hose down the house with the fifties? His chance of survival was low. The answer came. They needed or wanted something from him. What, he had no idea.

"I'm waiting for your reply. You're not going to let this lovely, well, not so much anymore, but this lady die because you're a coward, are you?"

Behind the general standing behind a jeep was a man in a gray suit and a woman in a long blue skirt and white blouse. Who were they? Members of the new government? Military intelligence? Their presence added a new dimension to whatever was happening here. They had the look of authority and power. Were they the ones pulling the strings? If so, they were the ones who abused Rose and were now using her to bring him out. They felt he had enough value to negotiate his surrender.

For a moment he considered giving up if only to get close enough to those two politicians to snap their necks. However, he knew the likelihood of getting the chance was close to nil. No, he only had one choice and it meant the death of both Rose and him. So be it. They were warriors. Violent death was at the end of the road for all of those like him.

Decision made, he lined up his shot. As Rose's image settled between the reticles, he was surprised to find the image before him clouded. Then he realized his eyes had filled with tears. Weatherman cared for Rose. In his own way loved her. He could not be the one to bring about her death. No. If she was going to die, it was not going to be by his hand. He blinked away the tears. These assholes had crossed the line and made it personal. They had no code. No honor. They would all die for the mistake.

"Okay, I guess we have to do the countdown thing. I'll be generous and give you till the count of ten. One. Two."

Weatherman sighted once more on Rose, knowing it was the last image of her he would have to remember. Before he could do anything else, her eyes forced open, and she nodded. Her lips changed her mantra. He struggled to understand them until he realized there were three distinct forms to her lips. *I. Love. You.*

"Three. Four."

The tears came again, and her words changed back to *kill me*.

"Five. Six."

Weatherman lowered his head, cleared his eyes, then focused on the scope. He acquired his target, said, "Forgive me, Rose," and broke the trigger.

The head recoiled slightly from the impact, then the general fell.

The stunned silence that followed gave Weatherman the chance to target and send the next round downrange. The man holding Rose on the left fell. Whether from lack of strength or because she knew it was smart, Rose dropped.

In the next second, war began. Bullets flew from every direction. The rattle of the fifties blocked all other sounds. The heavy rounds tore into and through the bricks and pocked the drywall with large holes.

Weatherman dove for the floor and crawled into the hallway. He dragged a heavy wooden dresser in behind him and shoved it against the interior wall. Then he pressed a mattress against the dresser and made himself as small as possible. The fifty caliber rounds had to pass through a brick wall, an interior wall, a dresser laden with clothes, and a mattress to get to him. He had no illusions about the possibility.

Even as he considered the odds, a drawer splintered and pain erupted in his arm. His only hope for survival was if they ran out of ammo before hitting him. As chances went, it wasn't likely, but he had nothing else to hope for.

PART 3

Chapter Twenty-Six

Sarge led them down Exchange Road out of the Village of Crete. They drove for twenty minutes down the winding road until they reached the Indiana-Illinois border. There he turned south on Stateline Road. Whether he had a plan or was just guessing was anyone's guess, but Jerome knew better than to challenge his lead.

Sarge slowed at intersections to scan their length, then drove onward. Whatever he was looking for was not down those roads. When he came to a road named Bemes, he turned west. At that point, Jerome wanted to know what the older man was thinking. He drove up next to the van and gave a one-handed shrug. As anticipated, Sarge frowned and ignored him. Jerome dropped back.

At Stoney Island Avenue, he turned south then pulled into a fire protection complex for Crete and the surrounding areas. By the time Jerome got off his bike, Sarge already had the map open over the hood of the van.

When everyone had gathered except for Merri, Sarge began. "Here's where we are." He pointed. "Here's Crete and this is the general area where we saw the jeeps. If this is a military-style operation, they will need a base. Depending on their numbers, which is an unknown, there are good options. I'm guessing if they have the sort of vehicles and numbers we saw on the streets, then the opposing force is large. That limits the choices for bases to the high school football stadium across the street, the horse training grounds here, or that complex of buildings in the oval over there.

"Since there is no activity at the stadium, we can eliminate that one. Also, because we have seen no patrol lights on the road once we left the Crete area, I think we can cut this one from the list." He pointed at the horse training grounds. That leaves this grouping of buildings."

Sarge glanced from face to face at that point, looking for questions or comments.

"That's taking a lot into assumption," Moore said. "There're miles of open ground around here. They could be on any of these farms or several if they were trying to control an area."

"Valid point," Sarge said, "however, we have seen no activity on this side of Crete. So, either they are working from one central location or the area they are trying to control is further west."

Moore nodded at that. "Okay, but whatever we do until we know more, we should proceed with caution to avoid driving right into the middle of them."

"Agreed."

Sarge looked at Jerome. "Anything?"

"Yeah. If we're that close to their base, I think it's time for me to ditch the bike. It's too loud. We don't need to draw them to us."

"Unless we want to do that to set a trap," said Moore. "If we capture one of them, we can press them for information."

"We can go that route if we choose," Sarge said.

"I think we hide the truck and the bike," Jerome said. "Leave one person to guard them and the rest go off to explore. Until we know more, we can't do anything. I'd like to find Weatherman and his people before the enemy finds us." He pointed at the lot. We can hide the truck in one of the bays the firetrucks are in and take one of the cars in the lot."

"So, leave everything then," Sarge said.

"Yeah, that's a clever idea," Moore said.

Sarge looked at them. "I'll stay."

From inside the van, Merri moaned loudly.

"How's she doing?" Jerome asked.

"We had a nice chat during the drive. We have an understanding. She's going to go through her withdrawals and never touch drugs again, or I'll leave her cramping and in pain on the side of the road to die alone."

"You're a hard man, Sarge."

"Just hard enough, son. Just hard enough."

"Can you handle her, or you want me to watch her?"

"No. I'll stay. She and I still have work to do before she can be salvaged."

Jerome studied the man. As much as he hated drugs and those who dealt and used them, he didn't think Sarge would do Merri harm. She had garnered grudging respect from the man with her actions back in Crete. "Okay. Let's set a time limit. We'll go out for two hours. If we're not back by then, we hit trouble. You should take Merri and go."

Sarge nodded but said, "We'll see."

Jerome smiled. "Fine. Do what you think's best. Let's get everything inside before someone stumbles across us."

Moore's friend got into the fire station. Since nothing was broken, Jerome assumed she had skills in that regard. She rolled up the large overhead door and Moore drove the truck into the unoccupied bay.

Jerome parked the bike inside along the wall. They had to open the second bay for the van. Sarge parked in front of an ambulance. They searched the building and found car keys in lockers situated upstairs above the bays.

They opted for a black Chevy Blazer. They chose the SUV in case they needed to go off-road. After loading gear and weapons, the Asian woman and Moore got in front, and Jerome slid into the back seat. The woman was driving and Jerome had to wonder what her role was: bodyguard, chauffeur, partner, lover, all the above?

She turned south down Stoney Island Avenue at a speed that allowed for time to maneuver should the need arise. It was midmorning and the sun was bright, allowing them to see a good distance across the open farmland. Jerome kept watch behind them so no one could sneak up.

As they drove, Moore asked. "So, who's the junkie in the van? A new girlfriend or just someone you're trying to save?"

"Merri's good people, AS. She's Coast Guard. She worked hard for command of her own boat. Got passed over and took it hard. I've been checking on her over the past few weeks and her mood had darkened. Don't know if there was a final breaking point, but she's hit bottom. I wasn't going to let her go without an effort."

"So, nothing romantic then."

Jerome looked away. "No. Nothing like that." He'd wanted there to be more and for a while thought that might happen, but then the pass over on the boat occurred, followed by the virus and he hadn't seen her since. The last two times he went to her apartment she was gone.

"So, what's the deal with your personal assistant?"

"You mean, Syn?"

"Wouldn't know since no introductions have been made."

"Oh, I think you got yourself an admirer," Moore said to the woman.

She flicked an irritated glance in the mirror, catching Jerome's eyes. He doubted the woman knew how to smile.

"Jerome, my friend, this is Syn Li."

"No doubt," Jerome said.

"I bought her freedom from a Triad leader when I was in San Francisco. They had trained her to be an assassin. She had failed a mission, and they were punishing her by abusing her in any way they saw fit. I stepped in and gave the man a choice. Die or sell her to me. He chose the better option."

"And they let her and you walk away?"

He laughed. "Hardly. Once they had my money, they tried to have me killed. If Syn killed me, all would be forgiven. She put a knife to my throat as the leader watched, then she pulled it back and threw it. The leader had enough time to be shocked by the knife protruding from his eyes before he died. We fought our way out and Syn Li and I have been kicking ass ever since."

"How long ago was that?"

"Not long. Four months. She doesn't speak much English, but we managed to strike a deal. She'd stay with me in whatever capacity I needed for two years to pay the debt—her idea, not mine, and then she was free to do as she pleased. I give her a salary, but she has yet to cash a single check. Says that's not fair to me. Says I already paid her in advance when I bought her."

"You gonna let her go when the two years are up?"

Moore turned to face him. "What kind of question is that? Of course, I am. In fact," he turned to Syn Li, "Syn."

She glanced at him.

"I release you from all debt. You are free to go."

She frowned at him but kept driving.

He touched her arm. "Syn, listen. You may not speak the language that well, but I know you understand me. I'm serious. Stop the car."

She gave a questioning look.

"Seriously, stop the car."

She braked and coasted to a stop.

"You are free to go. You can get out and leave right now if you wish."

She looked around, snorted a derisive laugh, and pointed out the window. She shrugged as if saying, 'and where would I go?'

"Okay. Fair point. The next place we go or whenever you want, you can leave. I promise. Just please, say goodbye first."

She put a tender hand on his cheek, gave an eerie smile, then slapped his face. "No." Then she held up her hand and snapped the thumb and next two fingers together to indicate, *close your mouth.* She pressed the pedal and they moved on.

Moore looked over the seat and raised his eyebrows. "I tried."

Chapter Twenty-Seven

They reached the first intersection and slowed. Moore aimed a monocular down the road. He spotted two farms and endless open land. Further down the road were two or three others. He saw no movement. He motioned with his hand for Syn to move on, then he heard something and held up a hand. Syn hit the brakes, throwing Jerome forward in his seat.

"What?" he said.

"Shh!" Moore stuck his head out the window. "You hear that?"

Moore slid to the passenger side and rolled down the window. "What do you hear?" Then he heard it. "Oh, gunshots."

"You think that's your friend?"

"No doubt in my mind."

"What do you want to do?"

"Let's see what's going on."

"Walking or driving?"

"Let's move to one of those farms and park there. We can decide once we're there."

Syn reversed and turned.

"This is Goodenow," said Moore. "It has to be them."

A half a mile later they pulled up behind a small farmhouse and then got out. They followed the direction of the gunshots. Jerome pointed a finger in a western direction, then tracked it toward the gun reports. "There." He put the glasses to his eyes. "Yeah, there's soldiers surrounding that house. Whoever they have trapped inside is holding his own. I see a half dozen bodies."

"Your call, my friend."

"Kit up. We'll make for the next farm, then go from there. It'll offer us better cover than crossing the field."

A minute later, they were moving along the street toward the bigger farm. They were still in the open but not in a direct line of sight. Most eyes would be directed toward the battle. It took fifteen minutes to reach the property. The ground offered no place to hide until they reached the buildings. Before they arrived, the door opened on the first structure. A man in uniform slid the barn door to the side. Seconds later, a Humvee exited. The soldier climbed inside and the vehicle tore down the middle of the grounds, around a house, and down a driveway toward the battle.

Minutes later, a jeep pulled up outside the barn door. Two men dragged a woman between them and lifted her into the back seat of the jeep. The two men bracketed her. A woman in a skirt came out and got in the passenger seat. The driver, a man in a suit, drove off. A hint of recognition sparked within Jerome. It took a second to make connections and the name came out. "Rose?"

"You know her?"

"Yeah."

"Well, she seemed okay. Are we in the wrong place?"

"Not the one in front."

"Huh? Oh! She was in bad shape."

"Yeah. We need to help her. She's part of Weatherman's team."

"Maybe he's in there, too."

"I was thinking that. Let's check."

They advanced in a triangle formation with Jerome in the lead and moved quickly across the grounds to the front of the stable. The door was still open. Jerome cleared entry while Moore and Syn watched north and south, then Jerome said, "Go," and entered. A Buick Enclave had been parked near the back. The building was empty of all life forms, human, horses or otherwise. They examined the area for clues.

Syn grunted and Moore moved to her. "Here," he said. Jerome joined them. A chair had been set up in a stall. Ropes hung from the back and legs. Blood-soaked straw covered the floor. "Looks like they tortured your friend," Moore said.

Jerome could feel the anger boil up within him turn to rage. He wanted blood too. It was time for war. "Let's move down the line and clear the buildings."

"What about the gunfight?"

"We can't join if we have enemy combatants at our six."

Moore nodded. "Yeah. Good point."

They turned to leave when a voice called out. "You freeze right there, or I'll drop you all."

Jerome glanced over a shoulder. A lone man stood at the half-open rear barn door with an AR aimed at them. If he had any skill at all, the soldier could do exactly as he said, especially at this close range. He wore a military combat uniform with an insignia he had never seen before.

"Drop your—Uh!"

The man's head snapped back and he dropped the weapon as blood ran from his mouth. He fell, leaving a woman with dirty, matted hair and a crazed look in her eyes standing there holding a bloody knife. She looked at them, her vision cleared, and she said, "Are you friends of Weatherman?"

The question startled Jerome.

"Well?" she demanded. "Yes or no. He doesn't have much time."

"Yes. I-we're friends of Weatherman."

"Okay. Come with me. Hurry."

Moore gave him a questioning look. Jerome gave a quick shrug and ran after the woman.

She reached the next stable and stopped. "Other friends of Weatherman are inside and covered by two guards. I only have a knife, so couldn't get close. They need to be put down fast. I'll free the others and we can go rescue Weatherman."

With that, she gripped the door and, much to Jerome's shock and panic, pulled it open. They had no plan, no idea of what or how many they faced, where they were positioned, or even the layout of the building. The door opened and two surprised men turned toward them. Jerome, Moore, and Syn opened up and cut them down before they got off a shot, but now every other enemy in camp knew they were there. He frowned at the woman. "Don't ever do that again."

She looked confused. He entered and found Money and two others he didn't know tied to posts. One was barely conscious. The woman rushed past them and began cutting through their bonds.

Money said, "Oh, God, Slicer, am I glad to see you. They took Rose and have been torturing her."

"We saw them load her in a jeep. She's gone."

As Money was freed, he stood. "Long Shot, Astronaut, and that's Ellie."

"We don't have time," Ellie interrupted. "They have Weatherman trapped in a house down the road. He's surrounded and if we don't help him, he's dead."

Jerome cocked his head and listened. "There seems to be a cease-fire at present."

"Negotiations," Money said. Then his head snapped up. "Did you see which way they took Rose?"

"South."

"They're using her to draw him out. We need to get there fast." He ran and bent next to the first guard, stripping his weapon. He got the AR and handgun but only one extra magazine for each.

"What about him," Moore said.

Money said, "No time. Astronaut."

Astronaut grunted.

"Come when you can. Otherwise, we'll come back for you."

He lifted a hand and dropped it.

Long Shot took the second AR, then turned and gave the handgun to Ellie. A surprised look crossed her blood-smeared face. "Well, you're part of this team, aren't you? Can't have you going into a fight without a weapon."

Money was already out the door. In front of him, two soldiers were running toward them. He never broke stride. He leveled the AR and fired, bringing both men down. Jerome followed but saw a man come out of the house to the right. He stopped, aimed, and took him down.

They ran past a Quonset hut and were faced with a quarter-mile of open ground. Ahead, a series of Humvees and jeeps were lined up in the field across from a brick ranch house. The two jeeps had mounted fifty caliber machine guns aimed at the house. As yet, they had not fired. Another jeep sat far to the left of the house. Two men held a woman he guessed was Rose. The suit and the woman in the skirt stood behind them. An officer held a gun to Rose's head.

Money turned, "Long Shot, that group there."

Long Shot broke right, dropped to the ground, and began adjusting his AR. Jerome assumed by the name he had mad skills as a sniper. Money veered left to keep Long Shot's line of sight clear.

Jerome caught up to Money. "We need to take out those fifties."

"That's you. Don't wait for a signal."

Money cut toward the jeep where Rose was, while Moore and Syn followed Jerome. Ellie followed Money.

They closed to within thirty yards when a shot was fired from the house. The resulting silence was the calm before the storm. The body of the officer hit the ground.

Three seconds later, the fifty-cals opened up in a staggered cacophony of death.

The bullets tore up and through the brick. If Weatherman wasn't already shredded, he soon would be. Jerome motioned to Moore to take the gun on the right. He moved further for the second gun. At ten yards from his target, he fired, seconds after Moore and Syn. Both gunners went down. The absence of their steady chatter was noticeable. Heads turned. They were standing in the open and had to reach the jeeps before return fire found them.

One soldier scrambled to the back of the second jeep. Jerome cut him down. The doors of the Humvee to the left of the jeep opened and men poured out. Jerome veered toward them, shooting the first two out before the next man closed the door.

Jerome leaped up onto the jeep in one long bound. He grabbed the machine gun, swiveled to face the Humvee, and pressed down on the firing mechanism. The gun roared to life, ripping through the protective glass windshield. The driver danced in his seat under multiple impacts, then he aimed through the front seats to the rear if only to force whoever was still inside to take cover.

The second machine gun came to life, cutting down the troops burrowed into the soft earth of the field. Moore was doing what he did best, killing. Jerome glanced right and was surprised to see it was Syn Li at the gun, not Moore. She seemed at one with the gun and the first sign of expression touched her face. Unless he was mistaken, it looked like pure joy.

Chapter Twenty-Eight

The troops broke not long after the machine guns were turned on them. They ran in all directions. Ellie ran for the house with no thought or regard for her safety. If Weatherman was still alive, he was just as likely to shoot her as an invading enemy as welcome her. Money ran after her screaming for her to stop understanding the possibilities better.

Long Shot arrived on the run. He spotted Rose and said to Moore with vehemence in his voice, "Watch those two." He pointed to the now cowering woman and man who had taken and tortured Rose. He squatted next to Rose. Her beaten, battered, and bloody body made Jerome believe she was dead. The sight and thought saddened him. Rose was a true warrior.

"Rose," Long Shot said softly as he cradled her in his arms. "Rose, can you hear me? You're safe now. We've got you." He felt for a pulse.

Her eyes fluttered open. To Jerome's surprise, she smiled. A weak hand lifted and patted Long Shot's face. "Of course, you do. I never doubted you'd come. Only your timing sucks." Her hand fell away and the smile faded into concern. "Weatherman?"

"Unknown. Money's checking."

"The bitch."

Long Shot knitted his brows, then he understood. "Alive, waiting for you to have a chat."

"Won't be much chatting."

"Might be good to know who they are."

"Help me up."

"You sure?"

She gave him a don't argue with me look and he lifted her from behind under the arms. He held her there for a moment as she stabilized, then stepped back. She took a deep breath and winced but fought through the agony. She forced her swollen eyes open. Blood seeped from multiple cuts and punctures. She looked like death—walking death, only she was the one about to bring it to her torturers. Her body straightened as if taking strength from the air.

From the house, they heard a scream. Ellie. "Weatherman," she shrieked.

They all turned and raised weapons save for Rose. They watched in silence, the tension thick and acrid like the expelled gasses over the battlefield. Long Shot positioned to have a clear shot at the house. Then Money poked an arm through the broken front window displaying a thumb's up and a collective breath was released.

With the issue of Weatherman's health settled, Rose spied her abusers pressed against the jeep and walked toward them. A whimper lifted from one of them. The woman steeled her gaze and stood to meet Rose. "You don't scare me. You're nothing."

"You must not be very good at your job since you couldn't even break nothing."

The woman began to speak. Rose lifted a finger and wagged it sideways.

"I'm not afraid of you." This time the words rang hollow.

Through her swollen, cracked lips, Rose smiled and barked a laugh. "Yes, you are." She whipped a backhand across the woman's face that staggered her. She emitted a cry of pain and put a hand to her cheek. Rose closed to within inches of the woman. A touch of fear now shone in the eyes. She fought hard to contain it. She straightened, placed her hands on Rose's chest, and pushed. Even weakened, Rose barely moved. She stepped in closer.

"Tell me, bitch, do you think you could stand up to the same torture you put me through?"

The woman stammered but did not form a response. Rose held the gaze for a long while. The others stood watching. Jerome was unsure of what to do. She turned and looked at him, then held out a hand. He knew what she wanted but hesitated. "You sure about this?"

Rose made a 'give me' sign with her fingers, and Jerome placed a blade in her hands. The corner of her mouth twitched. Jerome wondered if that was a thank you or a flicker of pain. He was an expert knife fighter in multiple techniques. He easily had more than fifty confirmed kills with a blade in one form or another, but he wasn't sure he could stand by and watch a woman be butchered alive.

Despite her wide range of injuries, everyone jumped at the flash of sudden movement. The blade made a quick but shallow slice in the woman's arm. She gasped and covered it. Blood seeped between her fingers and down her arm. An angry glare pinched the woman's face. She spat, "Do your worst, you little bitch. I should have carved my initials into your forehead."

Rose moved again, slicing into her other arm. "Who do you represent?"

"The government."

"Bullshit."

"You've been labeled a traitor." She swung her gaze to the others. "You're all traitors."

"We're not the ones who killed millions," Long Shot said. "You're terrorists."

"We do not recognize your authority," Rose said, stepping closer until her body pressed into the woman's. The woman retreated. Rose flicked her wrist and scribed a line across her abdomen, parting and staining the blouse. Rose moved fast, contacting the woman and driving her back against the jeep. She gripped the woman's hair, yanked it back, and drew a fine line across one cheek and down the other. Neither cut was deep. A streak of blood seeped from each as if created by a fine-tipped red pen. The sweet taste of satisfaction filled her as she saw tears build in the woman's eyes.

If Rose was aware of the crowd that had gathered around her, she did not show any signs.

Jerome said, "Rose," hoping to break her from the darkness that held her.

Rose snarled. "You see what she did to me? Look at me. She deserves whatever she gets."

"We're soldiers, Rose. This isn't what we do."

"That's right. We are soldiers. We put our lives on the line for a cause. What cause did she serve when she carved and beat on me? She had no purpose, no ultimate goal. She just enjoyed hurting me. What she did was wrong. I'm just balancing the scorecard." She turned to the woman and curled her lip. Venom dripped from her words. "You deserve far more than I want to spend time doing." She placed the tip of the blade on the woman's forehead and pressed slowly. The woman then broke, sobbing and pleading.

Rose pressed harder, parting the skin and boring into the skull. A large hand covered Rose's and held the blade in place. She looked back, rage darkening her face. Weatherman stood there, one arm bandaged and in a makeshift sling. He gazed at her with tenderness. "You're a warrior, Rose. We fight. We do not torture. You want to shoot her, you have the right, but this—this is not you. If you proceed with this, it will haunt you for the rest of your life. Believe me, I know."

"Look what she did to me." Her voice was almost pleading.

Weatherman nodded. "It's not right, but this doesn't even the score. It puts it in the negative for life. Don't cross this line. You're better than this—better than her."

Tears welled in Rose's eyes. She tipped her head back and roared with all her might at the sky. Weatherman said his piece. He removed his hand. It was Rose's choice now. She turned her gaze on the woman and then pulled the knife away. She spat in her face and allowed Weatherman to lead her away.

The woman cried harder and sagged to her knees.

Behind them they heard, "No."

They turned to see the Asian woman who arrived with Slicer standing next to the woman. "She do?" she motioned at Rose's face and body. Rose eyed her, then nodded.

"No live." Before anyone could react, Syn Li grabbed the woman's head, yanked it back, and carved through her neck so deep it exposed vertebrae. She threw the woman to the ground, then took out her handgun and fired a bullet into the head of the man in the suit. She looked at Rose and nodded. "Now, right."

Rose nodded back.

Chapter Twenty-Nine

As they walked back to the farmhouse, Money took control of the group. "Long Shot, see to Astronaut. Slicer—"

"Slicer?" Moore asked.

Jerome frowned at him and turned his attention to Money.

"You and Ellie take Rose—"

"I'll help Weatherman," Ellie said with finality.

"You do what you're told," Weatherman told her. "Help Slicer with Rose. She needs you more than I do."

Ellie scowled but took control of one side of Rose, and they helped her toward the stables.

Moore whispered something to Syn Li and she ran to the house.

Money started to speak to Moore. Moore stopped him.

"Don't know you and mean no disrespect, but I like doing my own thing. After we clear the house and the buildings, we've got another part of our team waiting for us a few miles from here. We're going to borrow a jeep and go get him." He gave a fake smile. "If that's alright with you."

It was clear he wasn't asking permission. Money didn't bother with a response. Moore smiled broader and went to clear the Quonset hut.

They drew even with the helicopter and Weatherman stopped. "Hold on a second," he said. He pulled his sidearm and moved toward the open cabin door.

Money stood to the side and leveled his AR to give cover. Seconds later, Weatherman said, "Come out of there." A muffled voice replied. "I'll kill you for sure if you don't come out."

Weatherman backed away, and a man slid out. He stood on nervous legs like he had to pee. His eyes flitted from Weatherman to Money.

"You're the mechanic." It was a statement.

"Y-yes, sir."

"Relax. I'm not going to hurt you." He holstered the gun to show he meant his words. "You have a valuable skill and didn't try to kill us. I don't make a habit of killing unarmed men. What's the condition of the bird?"

"Ah, I just need to change out a line. Other than that, everything checks out."

"Do you have the line you need?"

"No. It takes a special type and length and I didn't bring any with me."

"Is there anything comparable here on the farm you can use?"

The man appeared to give that thought. Well, it's a hydraulic line. It must fit perfectly. Otherwise, it might give out when you're in the air."

"Any way of patching it?"

"Yes, but it will only be temporary."

"What would you use?"

"A sealant and a lot of tightly wound tape."

"How long will that hold?"

"Unknown. The longer the use, the less the integrity. It will need to be changed again until the proper line can be found."

"Is there line anywhere nearby?"

He hesitated. "Yes, but it's back at the base."

"Listen to me. You need to repair it now. Get this thing ready to fly in the next thirty minutes. Understood?"

The man nodded. "When I'm done, are you going to let me go?"

Weatherman sighed.

Money said, "We're not going to kill you, but we won't let you go. At least not yet. You'll come with us until we can get a permanent replacement for the line. Then it will be up to you."

"What does that mean?"

"It means you have value. If you choose, you can come with us. Otherwise, once it's repaired, you are free to go. We will not kill you. You are no threat to us."

Weatherman said, "Let me say this though, if you purposely botch the repair thinking to bring us down, your life will end. Understood?"

The man nodded nervously.

"Get to work," Money said. "We'll be back shortly to check on you."

The mechanic scurried back inside.

Slicer's friends came out of their respective buildings. The man Slicer called Moore said, "All clear. We're going to take a jeep and get our friend. We'll be back in less than an hour, providing we don't run into any problems."

Money nodded. The man gave Weatherman a once over scan, then turned and walked toward the abandoned jeeps.

Weatherman said, "What was that about?"

"Always someone wanting to challenge the alpha dog," Money said.

Weatherman snorted. "I feel more like a whupped puppy."

"Maybe all the more reason." He glanced over his shoulder. "We should watch those two. I know they're friends of Slicer, but something feels off about them. Like they have their own agenda."

"Just what we need."

"Come on. Let me do a better job of treating that wound."

"I'd rather you saw to Rose."

"I will, but you're the easiest to clear. I'll work on her after I get you cleaned and rebandaged. She's going to take more work."

"What about Astronaut?"

"His wounds will heal, but I can't see what's going on in his head. He's got a concussion for sure. We should know more in time."

They entered the house in hopes of finding a first aid kit.

"We can't wait long. Those who escaped will get word back to their base. Others will come."

"We need the helo operational. You think we can trust the mechanic?"

"His life depends on doing the job. I plan to take him up with us. The look on his face will tell us all we need to know."

"We've got a lot to do," Money said.

"Well, then get started and stop gabbing."

Chapter Thirty

Jerome helped set Rose down, then did a scan of her injuries. There were a lot, but most were superficial. He turned to Long Shot. "We got any supplies to clean and bandage these wounds?"

"We might on the chopper."

Ellie volunteered to check. She ran off.

"She's part of the group?"

Long Shot gave him a strange look.

"She's not military if that's what you mean, but she's more than earned her spot. She came all by herself and rescued me and Astronaut. Unfortunately, it wasn't before he got roughed up." Astronaut was awake but in a fog. He had trouble forming sentences, losing track of the words before they were complete.

"Rose, how are you feeling," Long Shot asked.

"I hurt, but I'll survive."

"The wounds don't look bad, but there's a lot of them and a few look like they need stitches."

"Do what you can. I just need to be ambulatory. We can't stay here for long, or we'll be under attack again."

Ellie came back carrying a small duffel. "I found a bunch of stuff in here." She set it down between them.

"What's going on out there?" asked Long Shot.

"Ah, let's see, Money is finishing bandaging Weatherman. He said to tell you he'll be here in a minute. There's a really frightened guy working on the helo."

"I forgot it took some damage," Long Shot said. "Is it fixable?"

"He wasn't sure but was replacing or fixing a line. Oh, your two friends drove off," she said to Jerome.

Jerome nodded. They'd be going to get Sarge.

"Are you the one they call Slicer?"

"I haven't used that code name in a long time."

"I'm Ellie. Glad to know you."

Jerome smiled but didn't respond. He used an antiseptic to clean Rose's face and arms. With the skin clean, he could see the extent of the injuries. "The cuts on your face will heal but may leave thin scars. These two on your arms need stitches. The rest have mostly clotted already. I need to lift your shirt to see the wounds."

"Right," Rose quipped, "said every man to every woman."

Jerome smiled. Even in what had to be great pain, Rose was playing it cool.

"Go for it," she said.

Money entered and moved to Rose. "What do you got?"

"Two need closing on her arms. This one here across her abdomen might be okay, but it's long."

"Yeah, stitches. Anything more severe?"

"Haven't got to her legs yet, but the pants are caked with blood."

Money said, "Rose, I'm pulling down your pants."

"Always knew you just wanted an excuse to get in there."

"Yep, that's me. Lucky for you, we don't have enough time or the rafters would be shaking from your orgasmic screams."

She laughed and punched him. "That was good. Especially about having enough time. I'm sure we can spare the ten seconds you'd need."

He laughed. "Lift your hips." He started to slide her pants down, then paused. "Ellie, stand watch at the back door. Let's make sure we aren't taken by surprise. Slicer, would you help Long Shot get Astronaut to the chopper? If they do come for us, we won't have time to transport him during combat."

"Sure thing." He stood, knowing Money was trying to give Rose privacy, but the tasks made sense. He and Long Shot got on each side and hoisted Astronaut to his feet. They walked him from the stables. He wondered how long it would take for Moore and Sarge to arrive.

They reached the helicopter as the rotors began to spin.

"Looks like he got it working," Long Shot said.

Weatherman was sitting in the co-pilot's seat, talking to who Jerome assumed was the mechanic. The man was in the middle of an explanation when he climbed into the cabin. He slid Astronaut in and let Long Shot secure him.

"You lifting off?" Jerome asked.

Weatherman turned, "That's the plan. It's the quickest way to get distance."

"We hid the other helo at another farm about thirty minutes from here by air," Long Shot said.

"It works?" asked Weatherman.

"It did when we left it."

"Okay. We'll head there first."

"You've got two of them?" asked Jerome.

"Yep, our own air force. Hey, Jerome, I wanted to say thanks for coming and saving our butts."

"It's what I do." He flashed a wide smile.

"Yes, you do." Weatherman extended a fist and Jerome met it with his. "Ah, tell me a bit about your friends."

From the tone of the inquiry, Jerome guessed Weatherman had reservations about Moore and Syn Li.

"Alonzo Moore, code name Alien Species, AS for short. Former street thug who became a Ranger. Once out became an entrepreneur and rich. He may be the toughest man I ever knew, present company excluded, though he may be your equal. Problem?"

"Not sure. The way he acted and spoke leads me to believe he sees me as a challenge."

Jerome remained silent. He could see Moore being like that and doubted Weatherman was far off the mark. He bypassed a reply he knew his friend wanted. "Syn Li is just a stone-cold killer. Moore describes her as his assistant. I don't know how personal since I only just met her myself, but she does whatever he tells her to and if it involves violence, she does it with a smile.

"Now, Sarge, who they went back to get is a former Marine Master Sergeant. Took some heavy shrapnel to his legs and now walks with a limp. However, you never want to mention that to him. He is a proud man and will put even you down if you insult his integrity. He's a good man though old-fashioned and set in his ways."

"You know what we're up against, especially after witnessing what happened here. First question, are they in? Second, can they handle the pressure?'

Jerome knew better than to give a fast answer. Weatherman wanted and deserved the truth. "Sarge moves a bit slow, but he was the one who talked *me* into coming. He'll be an asset and can fight. Moore is as dangerous and deadly a man as you, and I say that with no exaggeration. I'm not sure about his commitment and believe he has an ulterior motive for leaving Chicago. Still, in a fight, there is no one better to have at your side. And Syn Li is ruthless. This might be a small group, but from the looks it will be quite formidable."

"Okay, good enough for me."

A cry of pain came from the stables. Weatherman started to move. Jerome put a hand on his arm. "Rose needs stitches. I think Money has begun sewing her up."

Weatherman nodded. "Hope he doesn't hurt her too much. We might end up one person short when he takes off."

"How do you want to work this? We have a van and a truck coming. Both are full of supplies and weapons."

Weatherman gave that some thought. "We might have to do air and land. We can send one bird off to scout and the other can cover the convoy."

"Do we want to take one of the Humvees?"

"Other than using up gas, it might be smart. I wish one of them had a fifty-cal attached. You want to pick one?"

"Yeah, I can strip the others while I'm there."

"Oh, you bastard," Rose shouted.

"Uh-oh!" Jerome said.

"Nice knowing you, Money," Weatherman said.

Chapter Thirty-One

They were ready and making plans by the time the van and truck arrived. To prevent more voices from altering the plans, Jerome motioned for Moore and Sarge to stay in the vans, then rejoined the group inside the helo.

"Rose, can you fly?" asked Money.

"We've only got two pilots, and Astronaut's out of rotation, so I'm going to have to."

"We could leave the birds," suggested Long Shot.

"If she can do it, I'd rather have them," said Weatherman.

"What are we going to do about the second one?" asked Ellie.

"We can decide that when we get there," Money said. "The longer we're here, the more likely of an attack. We need distance."

"I'll drive the Humvee," Jerome said.

"I'll ride with you," said Money.

Weatherman made a circle with his finger and Rose started the rotors whirling. They lifted off and cut cross country, leaving the convoy to find their own route. They found the second helo right where they left it. Rose set down beyond the farmhouse and Long Shot got out and ran to the house.

He knocked but got no response. He then pressed his face to the window. He returned minutes later after circling the house. "I don't think John and Addie are home. I hope they're alright."

Weatherman had the mechanic out looking at the second Black Hawk. He pointed underneath. "It looks like the landing wheels have caused some damage. Someone landed hard. It caused a crack in the underbelly of the fuselage."

"Is it safe to fly?"

The mechanic shrugged. "It will fly. However, it may not survive another landing, especially a hard one."

"Let me ask you something. Can you fly one of these?"

The man's shoulders slumped as if in defeat. "If I can, does that mean you're not going to let me go?"

"Look, we're not going to hurt you, but even if you can't fly, we're going to keep you at least until we know one of them works. If you can fly the second and get us out of the area, then maybe you can take the line from this one and replace the bad one. If that's done, I'll let you go, and we'll be on our way."

"God, I wish I knew if I could trust you."

"That works both ways. I want to trust that you won't try to kill us by bringing one of these birds down."

"That would mean my death as well."

"True unless you want to be a martyr."

"Not me."

"Okay. Start it up, make sure it flies and we'll move on. Do you know how to disable the tracking?"

Again, the man hesitated. Weatherman thought the mechanic was probably hoping someone tracked and rescued him. "If they track us and send more helos after us, they're going to try to shoot us down. They won't care that you're on board."

He saw the mechanic's acceptance of that statement. "Yeah, I can do that."

"Okay. Get to work. We need both done before the trucks get here."

With Money guiding them, they followed. However, having to make squared off turns to the helo's direct flight path caused them to fall behind fast. They knew they were moving east and south and were able to keep the Black

Hawk in sight for a long way. When it descended, the location became guesswork.

Twice along the route, people tried to flag them down. Once, a woman missed the Humvee but got in the path of the van. Sarge swerved to avoid her, but Syn Li drove straight at her, forcing the woman to make a last second dive to keep from being flattened.

Ten minutes after losing sight of the Black Hawk, they found the farmhouse where they set down. Jerome pulled up the driveway to the rear to give the other vehicles enough room to do the same. He made a wide turn over the grass so the Humvee was facing the street.

Everyone got out and they watched as the mechanic worked on the two machines. Moore walked over to Jerome. "So, that's the famous Weatherman."

Jerome wondered where this was going. "Yep."

Moore was silent as he took the measure of the man. Moore was a tall, muscular man, but Weatherman was bigger. Where Moore was always calculating something and looked sinister, Weatherman always looked calm even though Jerome knew his mind was working, taking in, and storing information. He started to understand why Money and Weatherman questioned him about his friend. Moore had something on his mind.

"Tell me, Slicer," he dragged the name out. Jerome had never told anyone his code name once he was out of the military. During their brief time together in the jungle survival training course, he had never offered a name or code name. "You think I could take him?"

Jerome frowned and faced his friend. "I think even if you could, you'd be in no condition to celebrate the accomplishment."

Moore bobbed his head as he ran that through his thought process.

Jerome said, "Tell me you're not here to challenge him. Tell me you have a better motive for coming than something that stupid."

"What?" he touched his chest and sounded insulted. "Why would you ask me that? Don't worry. I'm not going to hurt your precious Weatherman. I'm here because of what you told me. The whole military coop thing."

"Man, I hope so. Life is already tough enough without you adding to the burden."

"Man, now you're just pissing me off." They were silent for a moment before Moore changed the subject. "So, why didn't you tell me about your code name?"

"It was part of another life."

"Man, I knew you were a badass. You could have told me. Hell, you never even used it during our training time. You ashamed of it or something?"

"Well, now you know, and no, I wasn't ashamed. Just private."

"So, how'd you get that handle?"

Jerome looked at him. "How do you think?"

"You tough with a blade? Is that it? You know Syn Li is about the best I ever saw with one. You think you could match skills?"

"What is with you and all these challenges?"

"Alright, okay, don't get your panties in a bunch. Just playing." He changed topics. "So, what's with the chick?"

"Who? Rose?"

"No, man, I know she's the real deal. The other one. The one with the goo-goo eyes for your boy."

"Ellie's a civilian. That's all I know."

The rotors began to spin.

"You all tier twos?"

"No. Weatherman was tier one. I think Money was too, but not sure. The rest are twos."

Weatherman spotted them and strode over. "We're ready to go. We need to set up a meeting place in case we get separated."

"Sarge has a map," Jerome said. "Let's check with him."

As if anticipating the question, Sarge was already pouring over the map as they arrived. Before the question was posed, he pointed and said, "I'm thinking here's a good place to meet. It's a small airfield where you might be able to refuel those Black Hawks."

Weatherman said, "Good pick. I'm Weatherman," he said, offering his hand.

"Call me Sarge." He took it in a firm grip. He went back to the map. "We're not going far, but who knows when you can fuel up again. You've got two choices. Here, Lowell Airport and a little to the northeast, Wietbrock Airport."

Weatherman studied them then said. "We'll fly to Wietbrock but meet you here," he said, finishing at the Lowell Airport.

"Makes sense," Sarge said and began folding the map.

"See you there," Weatherman said. He turned and jogged toward the second Black Hawk.

Jerome said, "Sarge, how's your passenger?"

"Sleeping now, which is a good thing. Not sure how much longer I can put up with that moaning and groaning, or the smell."

"Let's get her through it, Sarge. She's good people. Trust me. She's worth saving."

"Hope you're right."

As they walked back to the vehicles, Jerome became aware of the cold silence emanating from Moore. "Man didn't offer me his hand. I feel slighted."

"He's not like that. Don't make a big deal out of this."

"I do."

Moore didn't answer, but he was upset over the perceived slight.

Chapter Thirty-Two

They drove out with Sarge in the lead. The two Black Hawks were already skyward. Jerome questioned Money about what he had learned regarding the virus and the government takeover. By the time Money was done answering, Jerome was speechless. To discover elements of his own military, a military he had spent so many years a part of, engaged in the conspiracy was too hard to believe or take. Millions had died for them to put their heinous plot into action.

By the time the discussion had run its course, Jerome was determined to do whatever was in his power to bring the traitors down. Those millions of lost souls demanded and deserved justice.

They arrived at Lowell Airport a little more than an hour later. It had a grass runway, one small hangar, and two metal buildings that offered service. Several storage buildings were on the property, as well as three houses. They drove down a long drive that ran between the houses and buildings and went around the hangar to the airfield side to be hidden as much as possible from the roads.

They exited and stretched. Sarge said, "I suggest that we eat while we have a chance."

"Sounds good to me," Jerome said.

Moore nodded and moved to the rear of the truck.

Jerome said, "Sarge, you didn't happen to think to unload the saddlebags on the bike, did you?"

"Please, boy, who you talking to? You'll find all your stuff stacked near the back, including that sweet sawed-off you had stashed."

"You're the best, Sarge."

"Ain't that the truth? Oh, and I think your lady friend is awake."

Jerome ignored the comment and followed Sarge to the back of the van. He opened the door and Merri screeched. "The sun. It's too bright."

"Come on out of there, young lady. Come face the day and your punishment. You're on the road to recovery and the toll will not be denied."

She curled into the fetal position and moaned.

"Nope. Not happening." Sarge grabbed her ankles and yanked her to the edge of the floor. She kicked and squealed. "At least she's got some life to her," he said to Jerome. To Merri, he said, "Come out, or I will yank you out. I'm not gonna care if you bounce that skinny bottom on the ground. Your choice. For some strange reason, this usually intelligent young man is of the opinion you're worth saving. I don't see it myself, but if you don't want him to be made a fool of, I suggest you get on out here."

"Alright. Alright, you old bastard. Get off me." With her face scrunched up against the brightness of the sun, she scooted to the edge and let her feet dangle.

"You're gonna have to do better than that. I need to get in there."

Jerome held out a hand. Merri looked as if she might slap it away but took it and allowed herself to be pulled out of the van. Standing was a problem as severe stomach cramps racked her. She doubled over and groaned.

"It will get worse before it gets better, Merri, but it will come to an end."

"You should have just left me to die."

Jerome grabbed her roughly by the shoulders. "Listen, you fool. You have survived when millions of others have not. For whatever reason, you made it. Stop treating your life as expendable. It is not. Whatever you went through before no longer matters. There is no Coast Guard, no command authority for you to listen to. No one to pass

over you, no boats to command. It's just you and every breath you take beyond the ones that killed everyone else. Now stop behaving like the universe is against you because there's not much of it left, and stop acting like you don't matter cause you do."
"Merri smiled at him. "You still care."
Before he could reply, she vomited all over him.

"Nice speech," Moore said as Jerome pulled fresh clothes from his duffel. "I thought it was anyway. Your girlfriend had a lower opinion of it."
"You're a funny man."
"I know, right?" He leaned against the van and crossed his thick arms. "Look, I want to apologize for my behavior. I'm not here for a personal agenda. The truth is it was getting too hard to protect my building in the city. It was safer to leave. If I can help with this conspiracy problem, then that's cool. We okay?"
"Yeah, man, we're good."
Before the conversation continued, Syn Li ran up and pointed beyond the buildings. The expression on her face told them whoever was coming wasn't someone they knew.
"Soldiers?"
She shook her head and ran off.
"Look alive, people," Moore said. "We got company."
Jerome and Moore ran to the rear of the hangar. Moore stayed on the near side while Jerome moved to the next one. From there, he had an angle on the two cross streets. Three pickup trucks and a delivery van were barreling toward them. They turned down the road which was across a field fifty yards from the airport. Once level with the hangar, the vehicles went offroad and cut directly toward them, leaving huge tire gouges in the soft earth.

He could see three people in the back of one truck and two in the cab of each. Two were in the front seats of the van too, but he had no idea if more were inside. He counted eleven bodies for sure—a far cry from a military assault but dangerous nonetheless.

Two trucks turned in between the hangar and the service buildings. One truck and the van pulled sideways to their vehicles, perhaps attempting to block them. Since the ground to the right of the vehicles was open, it was silly to try. The only other reason to park them in that formation was to use them as cover, which told him the predetermined direction this meeting would go. Doors opened and men piled out, each carrying a rifle. Most were scoped hunting rifles. He spotted two ARs and an AK47.

Though he had no vantage point to see who exited the van, since the sliding door opened, he knew someone was inside. Jerome figured three, putting the total opposition at fourteen.

One of the men shouted, "Who's in charge?"

No one answered. They couldn't know the number that stood against them. His thought was to let them come to them. It gave them a chance to even the odds a bit.

"I know you're there. We saw you drive up." The slight southern accent had a sing-song quality. "Well, I guess it don't matter none. We're going to take your stuff anyway. Just a matter of how many of you gotta die to make the transfer. You let us have the vehicles and no one dies."

A minute passed. The guy was getting pissed.

"Look, this is gonna go easier for you if someone talks to me. I'll tell you what we want, and the deal can be finished with no bloodshed. After all, you entered our territory. This is the price for invading us."

Another minute passed. Jerome could hear a heated exchange behind the vehicles as they tried to determine what to do and who was going to do it. "Man, if one of you shoots at us, it'll be a war zone and we won't stop until you're all dead. Last chance to do this civil like."

Moore said, "The guy talking is over here. You got anyone there?"

"Yeah. Got four here. Two are sneaking up along the building thinking they can sneak up behind us."

"You got 'em?"

"Yep." He walked away from the corner, let his AR hang from the sling, and pulled two throwing knives from their sheaths on the harness over his shoulders.

Moore whispered, "I think the guys on this side are waiting for your guys to get into position."

The first man reached the corner and peered around. He saw Jerome standing there with no gun in hand. He said something to his friend, then leveled his gun and stepped around the corner. He got one step when Jerome threw the knife. It struck him in the chest, an inch from his heart. The stunned expression showed the man hadn't yet registered the full extent of the damage done to him.

As the second man came around the corner, Jerome readied his second blade, but the man took a step and fell on his face, a long bloody gash was carved across his throat. Syn Li stepped forward. She had a karambit knife in one hand and a push dagger in the other. She glanced at Jerome's victim, then at him. She gave an approving nod and then was gone.

Jerome retrieved his knife and brought the AR back up. The two men at the trucks were gone. They must have figured the two dead men would flush them to the opposite side. That meant the way was clear for him to do the same. The problem was he would be in the open for a good forty yards.

With the weapon at the ready to fire position, he quickly walked toward the front, keeping an eye on the trucks and the corner of the building. Gunshots came from the other side. Moore had engaged. Where were Money and Sarge? He had an idea Sarge was in the van with Merri, but where was Money?

Movement to his left had him dropping to one knee and sighting at the target. Money came into view, highlighted through the scope. He must have gone into the woods behind the hangar and worked his way around. He reached the tailgate of the first truck, then climbed into the bed. Jerome continued moving. Money saw peripheral movement and pivoted toward Jerome. Jerome froze and pulled the AR away from his face to be recognized. Money nodded.

Jerome reached the corner and looked to Money for a signal. Money knelt behind the cab and lifted the lid of a large chrome toolbox. Jerome didn't understand what he was doing until he leaned on the roof to acquire a target. The lid offered cover from shots going through the front and rear windows.

He motioned Jerome forward. He moved to the rear of the second truck, then to the driver's side. Once settled, Money fired. Jerome pivoted around the tail and found men all in a line waiting to be mowed down.

Money put two down and Jerome shot one. The remaining men scampered for their vehicles. Jerome could have easily killed more, but let them go. He was pleased to see Money did the same. However, Moore ran forward, firing into the van and two pickup trucks as they drove away. Moore still had the Chicago streets in him. There you gave no quarter and expected none. He emptied the rest of his magazine into the last truck and was changing out another when Sarge came up and placed a hand on his arm and lowered it. With the heat of battle on Moore's face, he didn't like Sarge's interference. He pulled his arm away and glared at the older man. Sarge met the gaze unwavering, then Moore turned and walked away.

"Well, at least we have dinner," Money said, holding up a deer head.

Chapter Thirty-Three

The fresh kill had been gutted but not skinned. Money and Jerome spent time preparing the carcass while Sarge built a fire. Syn Li found and carved sticks for a spit, and within an hour, they had the venison cooking.

Before the meat was ready to eat, the trucks reappeared, this time with a larger convoy.

"Man," Moore said, "these crackers are messing with mealtime. They got no respect."

Sarge said, "No respect? Crackers?"

"What?" said Moore. "Was that offensive?"

"If you have to ask—"

Money said, "I wonder if there's a chance they'll negotiate."

"I think we should be prepared for no," said Jerome.

Moore looked longingly at the cooking meat. "If they make this meat burn, they're going to pay dearly." He took his knife, sliced a small piece that was still pink, and sucked it into his mouth. He released a low moan.

They moved into position. Jerome went back behind the hangar to the left side. He estimated over twenty shooters were coming for them this time. Considering the lack of a population, they had to represent most of the survivors in this area. Too bad many of them were going to die here today.

The trucks came straight down the driveway this time, then pulled up in a line front first at a slight angle. Bodies poured out of the vehicles, taking up positions behind the trucks and the cabs. They did not wait for talk. They just began firing. Jerome waited for the initial barrage to end. Such a waste of ammunition. If this apocalypse lasted, bullets would be in short supply as time passed. What they spent here would be a valuable commodity later.

He spied a group of men running toward the maintenance buildings to his left, an obvious attempt to flank them. He was sure that was where Moore and Syn Li had taken up position. That was verified seconds later as gunfire erupted. Sarge and Money engaged the group from the right side of the hangar. Jerome opted to stay in reserve to assist in whichever direction needed his support.

As the shooting escalated, Jerome decided on a different tactic. With all the attention on the far sides of the hangar and the maintenance building, Jerome took the opportunity to sprint across open ground to reach the next building. Though he drew shots, they were too slow to acquire him and not skilled enough to come close.

He continued running past Moore and Syn Li and into the woods at the edge of the property. He ran twenty yards deep into the trees before turning north another forty yards and then went east. As he moved, he kept looking through the trees to find the end of the line of trucks. He was too far into cover to make out anything but drew his information from the sound of the shots. Once they were behind him, he turned.

He reached the tree line and squatted behind a birch that did not offer significant concealment. He came out in line with the second maintenance building and to the right of a house. From there, he could make out the backs of the men behind the first two trucks. He sprinted to the side of the building and knelt, drawing a bead on the first man. He fired twice and the man fell. The second man saw his comrade fall and glanced around for the shooter.

Jerome pressed back to get out of sight. He gave the man thirty seconds before inching forward. His target had moved, afraid to be that close to a dead friend. Jerome reacquired him halfway down the building's length. He fired twice more and put down another enemy fighter. He backed away and darted into the woods. From there, he worked north until he came out behind the house. Though further away, the new position gave him a complete look at the opposition. One other man was down. A few were huddled, devising a plan of attack. They must have thought their sheer numbers would cause their opposition to flee. They picked the wrong group to try to intimidate.

 He noted a lack of firing from his side. Did that mean someone was down? No, he thought. It would take a very skilled or extremely lucky shot to hit any of them. They were all trained professionals and would not waste bullets without a purpose. Perhaps they were trying to lure the attackers out.

 Two of the men ran back toward the smaller house across the street from the house where he now stood. They had the same thought as him: work around the enemy through the woods. Jerome slid to the rear of the house and waited. His AR had a two-point sling which allowed him to slide it to his back and free his hands. He slid out a throwing knife and his combat knife and waited.

 The two men had to cross sixty yards of open ground to get from one house to the other. They would be winded, adrenaline spiked, and thankful to still be alive. They would slow once behind cover but would not stop. They'd move straight for the trees behind the house. With those thoughts in mind, he plotted his attack.

 He heard them long before they reached the house. The rattle of whatever they carried and the heavy breathing from their all-out sprint made their arrival easy to judge. The first man ran past and Jerome attacked the second man. He rammed the combat knife up under the rib cage from the left side, angling toward the heart. As he did, he yanked the body in front of him and cocked his arm. As the lead man turned to see what his partner's problem was, Jerome let the blade fly. '

Accuracy on a stationary target was easy to achieve with practice. Against a live, moving target, it wasn't always a sure strike. The blade hit the man in the chest and buried deep. It stunned and staggered the man but did not kill him. Unless up close and personal, it was difficult to get a killing throw. As the man lifted his rifle, Jerome shoved the first man forward. The collision knocked him back and off balance. He released the man, pulled another blade from his harness, and plunged it into the second man's throat. He gurgled, clutched at the knife, and finally, his knees buckled.

Jerome yanked the knife free as his opponent fell. Both men lay bleeding and dying. He didn't stop to feel sorry for them. It was war, one they started. People died in war. He collected his knives, slid the AR to the ready fire position, and moved to the side of the house.

The attackers had increased their rate of fire. Jerome figured it was to cover their two friends they expected to be sneaking up behind their enemies. They were going to be extremely disappointed. He sprinted across the street to the smaller house, went around back, and dropped to one knee. He acquired his first target, a thin, bald man at the end of the line. He popped off three rounds with two hits, none of them immediately lethal. The man went down writhing on the ground.

The man next to him stared at his friend, stunned but made no move to help him. He glanced around trying to determine where the shot came from. When he looked back at the house, Jerome triggered three more shots, and he went down. By then, the others knew something was wrong. Several scrambled for cover from both directions.

The battle intensified, though most shots came from the attackers. His people would wait for them to run low on bullets. One man climbed inside one of the trucks and fired up the engine. His partners shouted at him to stop, but he sped down the driveway between the two houses.

Jerome pivoted and stitched a line across the passenger window. The man jerked in his seat and the truck veered left, going off the road and smashed into a tree.

With their numbers dwindling fast, panic swept through the enemy ranks. The sound of the approaching helos added to the confusion and fear. Jerome smiled as Rose brought the Black Hawk in line with the row of trucks. Weatherman stood at the gun. The attackers didn't know what to do. Before they got themselves mowed down, Jerome moved forward and shouted. "Lay your weapons down, get in your trucks and leave."

It was hard for them to hear over the sound of the rotors, so he repeated his commands with a visual display of what he wanted. A discussion ensued with a lack of agreement. Jerome got irritated. He was trying to save their lives. He raised a hand and motioned to Weatherman, then pointed at the first truck. Weatherman sent a burst into the truck that caused the gas tank to explode. The truck lifted into the air in a ball of flames, sending deadly metal debris yards away. Some of the men were knocked off their feet. Others ran.

Jerome repeated his demand. This time many of them threw their rifles down and ran for the trucks. He had no desire to kill anyone else, but one man held onto his rifle as he moved toward a vehicle. Jerome fired into the ground near his feet. One of the bullets ricocheted off the blacktop and struck his calf. He squealed and fell, the rifle clattering away. One of the others jumped out of the truck with his hands raised and moved toward his fallen comrade. He helped him onto the truck and they fled with the others.

Jerome sighed. City, country, it made no difference. There were crazies everywhere just anxious to kill and dumb enough to die.

Chapter Thirty-Four

Rose set the helo down on the airstrip. The mechanic landed twenty yards past. Everyone except Syn Li joined together in a low-key yet happy reunion. The strange woman chose to stay out of sight.

When asked, Moore said, "Don't worry about her. She's making sure no one else is lurking about to make our lives interesting. She'll show up."

Sarge was working his makeshift spit. A sizable portion of the meat charred during the battle. Money and Ellie rummaged through the assorted food supplies to find side dishes to compliment the venison. Long Shot went through the houses, bringing pots, plates, and silverware and dragging a gas grill with him on his return. Money dumped five cans of baked beans into a pot and set it on the grill. Ellie opened three cans of green beans into a smaller pot and added a can of diced tomatoes.

With the meal ready, they all took a plate and helped themselves, then found seats wherever they could. Moore dug through his stores and came out with a case of warm beer. He passed them out to cheers and took one himself. As he sat on the rear bumper, Syn Li arrived. She sniffed at the meat, then ignored it, scooping out a helping of both beans. She sat on the ground next to Moore's feet.

The meal was consumed in silence. As they finished and settled back in a post-meal and post-battle state of relaxation, the discussion of what to do next began. Money and Weatherman drove the conversation.

"I think we need to know more about who we're up against and what their ultimate goal is," Money said.

"I'm not disagreeing," said Weatherman, "but we also need greater numbers and a secure base of operations if we're to take on whoever we're up against."

"And I agree with you. I just think the priority should be intel."

Rose said, "Do we all get a say in this, or is it just your two dicks vying for control?"

Weatherman looked at her and said, "No, your dick can have a say too."

Laughter greeted the reply. Rose snorted. "Well, good cause mine's bigger than both of yours put together."

"I believe that," said Moore.

Money said, "What's on your mind?"

"They are certainly aware of us by now and understand we are a real threat. I think we do need more intel, but if we're going to face these people, we'll need help. We can go around the country and gather key personnel, and we should, but that's time consuming. We need large numbers now. To do that, we need to show this new government for the murderers they are."

"Agreed," Money said. "You want to spread the word through the remaining population."

"Yes, but most of them will be unprepared to resist a new government. If they were willing to kill millions, they wouldn't hesitate to eliminate any who oppose them."

Weatherman said, "When I came for you in Georgia, I was captured for a short time by a militia border guard who told me it was futile to stand against them. The virus was only the first step in their plans and he mentioned Phase Two was about to begin. It would be nice to know what that is."

Sarge spoke for the first time. "I know you don't know me, and I may not be up to speed on what you all know, but it seems to me with the number of skilled professionals you have collected around you that we can do both."

Money nodded to him, "Go ahead."

Sarge said, "Well, let me ask you each a question." To Money, he said, "Do you have an idea of where to go to gather your intel?"

Money gave the question thought. "I think so."

To Weatherman, Sarge asked, "Do you have an idea of where to go to recruit more people?"

"Yes."

"Then I suggest we split the group into two. "You," he motioned to Money, "seek out your intel while also looking for recruits." He turned to Weatherman, "You find your recruits while keeping an eye out for intel. We set a time and a central meeting place. Once we rejoin, we may have what we need for *our* next phase or at least have a better understanding and idea of what to do next."

Money and Weatherman exchanged glances and they each looked around the group. Weatherman said, "Any other suggestions?"

"Yeah," said Long Shot. "I don't disagree with any of what's been said, but for the moment we should spend an entire day here. That will allow our injured a day of rest and will allow us to check inventories, decide on our missions and figure out our timeline and meeting place."

"I'm good with that," Weatherman said.

"Sure, got my vote," said Rose.

"Any objections?" asked Money

"I suggest we set up a watch," Jerome said. "We can bunk in the two houses and move the vehicles into the hangar."

"Rose, Astronaut, and our new mechanic friend can be excluded from the rotation."

Rose started to object, but Money cut her off. "No one's playing favorites here, Rose. You went through a severe and brutal ordeal. Your body needs time to recover, and you're our only combat-trained pilot. It's the right call."

The others backed up Money's words with nods and she relented.

Jerome said, "Set a two-person watch every two hours?"

Money said, "We've got eight, so four teams of two gives us an eight-hour block of downtime with six hours sleep each. We'll save an additional two-hour block while we finalize plans for any who needs extra rack time. That good with everyone?"

"Sarge and I will take first watch," Jerome said.

Moore said, "Syn Li and I will take second."

"You and me, Long Shot?" Money asked.

"Deal."

Weatherman looked around. "Ellie's eyes were bright with excitement.

Rose chuckled.

They still had several hours of daylight left. They moved the van and truck inside the hangar and Sarge and Moore went through the supplies of food, drinks, and ammo to organize and get an idea of what they had.

The mechanic did a thorough inspection of both Black Hawks. Weatherman asked, "What's the verdict?"

"The line is holding for now. A long flight may well cause a leak, but for now it's working."

"Both birds will fly?"

"Yep. I suggest however, that you make periodic landings to check them out. You'll need to refuel anyway. That may be the best time to examine the patch."

Money and Long Shot helped Astronaut to the larger house. They placed him on the bed in the smaller of the three bedrooms while Rose settled into the master. They checked Astronaut's wounds and changed out the bandages. Astronaut had deep puncture wounds in his legs that had them concerned. They had no idea what internal damage might have been done, but the greater fear was infection.

"We need to check our medical supplies for antibiotics," Money said.

"I'll do that when I get back to the vehicles. You should check on Rose. She took a beating and is not the type to complain or ask for help. We can't have her passing out while in the air."

After Long Shot left, Money stood outside Rose's door. He knocked lightly but got no response. "Rose, it's me." When she didn't answer, he cracked open the door and peeked. She was already out. He watched for a moment, then crept into the room. He didn't want to wake her and sure didn't want to startle her, but he placed a gentle hand on her forehead. It might have been the heat or that she just ate, but he thought she had a temperature. If so, it wasn't much, but it was something to watch. "Sweet dreams, Rose." He closed the door and left the house.

Chapter Thirty-Five

As the sun began its descent, Weatherman joined the group in the hangar sitting in an assortment of folding lawn chairs. A few had beers. Someone had made a pot of coffee on the grill. Mugs had been set on the sideboard. He helped himself, opened a chair, and dropped into it, feeling the extent of his exhaustion as his body relaxed.

He sipped and gazed at the dying fire in the pit. The meat had been stripped from the bone. He was sure it was packed and stored someplace. They couldn't afford to waste fresh food.

Money said, "We're set food-wise for several days but will need to find more. Water is in short supply and may only last a day depending on rationing."

"Did Long Shot find any antibiotics?"

"Yeah. He took them to the house."

Weatherman turned to Moore and Sarge. "I don't suppose either of you brought a ham radio with you."

Moore glanced at Sarge, then shook his head. Sarge frowned as if to say *Seriously?* Then he got up and went to the van. He came back a minute later with a handheld portable unit and a larger model.

"You're kidding me?" Weatherman said, standing up.

"Not in the least," said Sarge.

Moore said, "What? You a boy scout or something?"

"Good boy scouts grow up to be great Marines." He held them out to Weatherman. The larger model can be rigged to run off a car battery. I should have what we need to adapt the power. The smaller unit is charged and ready to go. I've got a fifty-foot antenna wire and a booster to send the signal farther.

"Let's try the smaller unit. Maybe we can get lucky and find some relays."

They taped a rock to the end of the antenna and flung it to the top of the hangar. Then Sarge fiddled with the dials until he heard voices. "We've got a connection though I'm not sure where it is."

Over the next thirty minutes, Weatherman tried to reach the six people on his list that weren't in his present company. He had previously spoken twice to Monster in Texas and once to Shaman in Arizona. Rotors, Voodoo, and Breeze had been unreachable. Through connections with other operators, he managed to get a scratchy connection with Voodoo in New Orleans.

"Brother, glad to hear you're still in the land of the living."

"Same. You doing alright?" Weatherman said.

"Was forced to bug out. Me and a few others from the Big Easy are on the road. We're heading to Georgia. There's supposed to be a militia forming there. Thought we'd lend a hand."

Weatherman looked at Money. "Voo-ah, Brother, you don't want to do that until after you've talked to us."

"And why is that, Weath—"

"Whoa! No names of any sort."

"Okay. You got me intrigued. What's the haps?"

Money motioned with his hand, and Weatherman gave him the radio. "Listen, Brother. This is a distant friend from the disco dance club. Think hard."

It took a second, and then it came to him. "Oh, the Saturday Night Staying Alive, Dude. Yeah."

"Listen, Brother, this is important. There's lots you need to know before you go signing up. Can you hole up and wait for my arrival?"

"This sounds important and I remember you as a serious dude. You've got my ears perked, but I need more."

"I'll give more but when I see you. The waves are being scanned."

"This some conspiracy having to do with the pandemic?"

"Affirmative. Can you wait?"

"Let me discuss it with my boys."

"Do that. I'm on my way. This is urgent."

"I hear you. I'll get back to you."

"Roger." He ended the connection.

"Disco dance club?" Weatherman asked with eyebrows raised.

Money said, "During an ambush, I took refuge in a building where six seals were hiding. For some strange reason, a disco ball hung from the ceiling of this one-story building. Throughout the conflict, I kept humming the Staying Alive song, and it became a mantra we kept repeating until reinforcements arrived to free us. We were pinned down under heavy fire for eight hours and that stupid disco ball survived the entire encounter."

"So, you know him, then."

"Not other than that abbreviated time. Afterward, I was whisked away to make my report and never saw any of them again. Two of them took severe wounds. I never heard if they made it or not. But I remember the others referring to the code name, Voodoo."

"He's a fighter. Doesn't surprise me that he's ready to re-up. Some have trouble reestablishing a normal life after so long looking downrange. Does this fit in with your plan?"

"In a way. I wanted to go down near Georgia. I thought I could capture a few of the border patrol and interrogate them. I want to hear more about this Phase Two you mentioned, as well as whatever else I can learn."

"Michigan is one of the five conspiracy states and that's closer."

"That was my original plan, but this way, I can kill two birds—gather info and recruit. Ha, top that."

Weatherman smiled. "I'm going to try for Monster or Shaman, however, both live in Conspiracy states, Texas and Arizona. If the borders are closed, getting in might be tough. The Black Hawk might be the only way."

"You better make sure you can reach either of them before you go. We can't afford to get you shot down."

"If Texas is under their control, you better believe they have access to fighter jets and will put them to use. Also, since Monster is ex-military, it's likely he's already been recruited."

"I thought about that. He has a wife and daughter for them to use as leverage against him, too. Still, I need to try."

All efforts to reach Monster went unanswered. That didn't bode well for a positive outcome. He switched calls and managed to get a brief connection with Shaman.

"I am here. We have taken to the mountains. These amateurs they have sent after us will never survive."

"We're on our way. Hang tough."

"Always. You know where?"

"I have an idea. I'll get more when I'm closer. Might be a few days, though." For the benefit of anyone listening, he said, "Driving cross country these days is a dangerous undertaking, plus we have two other stops to make along the east coast. Look for me on the day of your sons. Go 1U for next." He shut down the connection.

"The day of your sons?" asked Money.

"He has two sons. Two days."

"Sounds like the plans have been made," said Sarge.

"We leave in the morning," said Weatherman.

"What's the split?" asked Money.

The truck and van can carry more. "Take Sarge, Moore, and his friend. I'll need Rose to pilot. If Astronaut can travel, I'll take him and Long Shot. Oh, and the mechanic to fly the second bird." He turned to Jerome. "Your choice."

"You've got two injured, one of which may not be of any use. I'll ride with you."

He looked at Money, who nodded.

"That everyone?" asked Weatherman.

Money frowned, then gave a slight sideways nod of his head. Weatherman followed the direction and spotted Ellie standing near the doorway. Though Long Shot was instructing her on how to adjust her sling, she was listening to the conversation. The hurt expression on her face told Weatherman all he needed to know.

"Hey, Ellie, you paying attention?" Ellie swept her sad eyes from Weatherman back to Long Shot. "This is a double sling which allows you to sweep it from front to back when you need to be hands-free. I adjusted it so it's tighter to your body and easier to manage. You need to practice to make the transition easy."

Weatherman lowered his voice. "I can't deal with this."

"She might be more trouble if you push her away," Money said.

"Can she fight?" asked Jerome.

Money said, "She's not trained, but she has been surprisingly useful."

"Will you be alright if I switch?" Jerome asked.

"We'll be okay."

"It might be for the best anyway. Merri is still in the back, recovering from her high. She might not react well if she wakes to unfamiliar faces."

"Merri?"

"Coast Guard. Going through a rough spot. She'll be alright."

Sarge said, "She'd better."

"Sounds like our teams are set. Let's divvy up the food and gear so we're ready to roll in the morning."

Twenty minutes later, they were on their way back to the houses. Money went to the larger house, while Ellie followed Weatherman to the smaller one. Sarge opted to stay with the van in the hangar.

The smaller house had two bedrooms. "Good night," Weatherman said, pushing through the door into one bedroom.

"Why didn't you want me?" Ellie asked, her voice soft and as fragile as a confused child's.

He faced her. "It had nothing to do with not wanting you. It's a matter of assigning the best people for each mission. Where we're going will be tougher than the other mission. The more skilled people should be with me. It has nothing to do with feelings or emotions. It's professional. Nothing more. Now get some sleep. Our watch will come up fast."

She started to speak, but he closed the door. He took off his boots, hoping with a watch stationed, he'd have advanced warning if another attack was coming. The queen size bed looked inviting. He pulled the covers back, sat, swept his legs up, and turned his back on the door. He had just begun to drift when he heard her enter.

She padded lightly to the bed and slid in next to him. He waited for her to make contact, expecting her to be naked. To his surprise, she curled up with her back to him. Minutes later, he heard the soft breaths like a cat's purr. She only wanted to be close. He was too tired to be concerned.

Chapter Thirty-Six

Jerome and Sarge did a lap together near the end of their shift. "Jerome, we've known each other for only a short time, but I've come to have great respect for you as a person and know I would've been proud to have you in my unit. In short, I trust you. That being said, are you sure this is the right thing for us to be doing?"

Jerome laughed. "If I remember right, you were the one who talked me into joining this campaign."

"Well, that's what you get for listening to an old fool. Since when did you ever listen to me?"

"It's not too late. We can pack and leave anytime."

"Would you leave your friends?"

Jerome thought about that for a moment. "If I never came, I wouldn't have looked back. However, now that I'm here, having been in several battles with who I now see as the enemy and knowing what I do, I don't think I could leave."

Sarge was silent for a while. "No. I don't suppose you can any more than I can. Doing what's right is just in our blood. It's one of the reasons I have such profound respect for you."

"As much as you say you respect me, I have that same respect for Weatherman. You can always trust him to do the right thing. If I had to pick a side, I'd always see which one he aligned with and follow suit. I can't say I know or understand what has happened to this country, but I trust that Weatherman will get to the core of the problem. We'll go from there as the story is revealed."

"What about this Money fellow? He sounds and acts like he came from Money."

"I can't say that I know him. I just met him the other day, but I've seen him at staging areas before one of our missions. I believe he was Army Intelligence and was then recruited into the CIA. I think he's a tier-one operative and spent time at the CIA's Special Activities Center on a SOG team."

"SOG? Special Operations Group?"

"Yeah, they do a lot of politically deniable clandestine missions."

"So, he's a spook."

"I guess."

"Can he be trusted?"

"All I've got to go on is he's with Weatherman. As far as that goes, see previous explanation."

"Just like to know who I'm going into battle with so I know if I can count on them to watch my back."

"Understood."

"Now, what about Moore and his friend? Will they follow directions and stick with the plan?"

Jerome hesitated before responding. "When it comes to a fight, Moore and his partner are more than qualified. Will he stand and fight? I don't know. He's not big on taking orders. He's more a free spirit doing whatever he thinks is right. He's a wild card."

"One more question? Why didn't you talk me out of me talking you into this insanity?"

"Hey, you're an old fool. You wouldn't have listened."

Sarge barked a short laugh.

The alarm on his watch went off and he woke in an instant. Ellie was still sleeping. She wore a relaxed and sweet smile. He crawled over her and donned his boots. He went to the bathroom and then came back to wake her.

She stretched languidly and smiled up at him like they were newlyweds. "Hey, get moving. We can't be late for our watch. It's not fair to the others."

She got up fast. And stood. She wasn't naked but had stripped down to her underwear. She gave a coy look as she pranced past him to retrieve her clothes from the other room. He decided not to wait for her. She ran to catch him. "Why didn't—"

He hushed her. With two roads to watch to the north and only one to the south, he told her to take up a position near the Black Hawks and to stay alert. He went to the northern section of the property and took a position in the trees at the far end of the third house. He had a clear vantage point to see anything moving along either road. He had sporadic starlight to see by, but it was always changing as the cloud cover shifted. The moon remained mostly obscured.

The time dragged. He forced himself awake and took a quick stroll. The streak of light in the sky from the east announced his watch was ending. They had spent a peaceful night. The jeep came from the west, appearing from behind the trees that ran to the road. Because the road angled northeast, he didn't think they were spotted. One Black Hawk was the only vehicle in the open and it was behind the hangar. However, if either person in the jeep glanced back, the lightening sky would reveal its presence.

He lifted his glasses and watched it grow smaller in the distance. The ground was open for a long way to the east. If the jeep turned around and came back, they would be spotted. Once the jeep was out of range, he ran to the house. He entered fast and shouted. Up! Up! Bug out in ten."

Weatherman didn't wait for them to rise and he bolted from the house and went to roust the others.

Sarge was already awake and making coffee.

"No time," Weatherman said. "We've got company."

As the others came awake, he told them. "A lone jeep moving toward the northeast. Not sure of its purpose.

Could be a scout moving toward Michigan, or it could be an advance team ahead of a column. Whatever, it's time to leave. Has everything been distributed?"

Sarge said, "Last night."

"Mount up. Try to stay behind the hangar in case anyone else passes."

A burst of activity came from everywhere at once. Money and Long Shot arrived, helping a now awake Astronaut between them. Rose jogged straight to the helo. Moore and Syn Li climbed into the truck. The engine came to life.

After depositing Astronaut in the Black Hawk, Money ran back with Long Shot, who said, "I told Ellie to stay in the helo with the mechanic."

Money said, "You all set?"

"Yes," Weatherman replied, "but we never discussed where to meet or when. How long do you think you'll need?"

"Two days down providing no hiccups, one to meet with your friend and his people, two to gather info, and two more to reach wherever we're meeting."

"We need a safe area away from the conspiracy states. Something midwestern. Kansas maybe."

"There's a small town north of Wichita called Park City. One week from today."

"You take Sarge's handheld radio. Stay off the air unless it's urgent."

"Done." Money extended his hand. Weatherman gripped it and pulled him close. "You be safe."

"And you." They released and Money ran to get the radio from Sarge.

Long Shot ran for the helo which Rose had warming up. The mechanic was just getting his bird started

Jerome was the only one left not mounted. "I'd like to say it was good seeing you again, but every time I see you, it means there's a fight brewing."

"This one may be the biggest and most important fight of our lives. Good luck to you. Help Money all you can. He's as top-notch as you are."

A low rumble sent a vibration through the ground.

"What the hell is that?" Jerome asked.

"Jesus," Weatherman said, "it's a tank."

Chapter Thirty-Seven

Jerome's eyes widened. He ran for the Humvee. Sarge sped out of the hangar. The truck was already moving, but Syn Li appeared unsure of where to go.

Weatherman ran for the furthest Black Hawk. With its rotors spinning and the sun cresting the horizon, it was easier to see.

The only paved surface for the truck and van to travel on was the driveway which connected to the road the tank was traveling on. Though still blocked from view by the trees, the increased vibrations told him it was getting closer. They had no chance for Sarge or Syn Li to reach the road and escape before the tank arrived. Their only chance of escape was to cross the soft dirt field and reach the southbound road beyond.

Jerome hopped out of the Humvee and sprinted toward the truck. He leaped on the passenger side step and yelled to Moore, pointing across the field. Syn Li turned sharply and drove in that direction and Jerome jumped down and returned to the Humvee. The truck started across, but the change of direction bled off much of its speed. As a result, the tires hit the grass, then the soft dirt and began to bog down. The van had gathered enough speed and was lighter and plowed through. The Humvee had no trouble.

Sarge sped down the road, but Money held the Humvee back until the truck made it across. The first Black Hawk lifted off and flew south. The second struggled under the pressured and inexperienced mechanic but climbed. It had just reached treetop height when the first enemy vehicle cleared the tree line.

A Humvee proceeded the tank. It spotted the truck and slowed. The tank came into view with the truck straining to cross, but it was still moving. With the houses in the way, the truck and van were blocked from the tank's line of sight for precious seconds. A column of other vehicles followed.

Though it was an older model tank, Weatherman didn't doubt its destructive power. "We need to draw their attention away from the truck," Weatherman said. "You up to it?"

The mechanic looked terrified. The second helo banked and came back, perhaps anticipating the mechanic's fear and lack of combat experience. Rose waved them on and flew past them, heading toward the tank.

The top hatch was open and a soldier had glasses up to his face. He spotted the truck and was busy giving instructions as the Black Hawk dove at him.

"Hold steady," Long Shot said. "Ellie, take the machine gun."

Rose leveled off. Though not still, the Black Hawk was steady enough to get off a short burst from the fifty caliber. The officer froze for an instant, then grabbed the hatch. Long Shot's bullet took him through the arm and must have hit bone because the arm collapsed at a strange angle. The hatch struck his head, driving him and his scream inside the tank.

The turret swung their way. Ellie swiveled the machine gun. She had basic training but had never fired the weapon. Her initial wild burst didn't come close to the target. Rose couldn't wait for the turret to acquire them, and she banked left and moved over the trees.

She flew wide before turning back toward the column. They discovered troop and cargo carrying deuce and half trucks, Humvees, and two more tanks in the column.

Long Shot replaced Ellie at the fifty-caliber machine gun and once Rose came broadside to the convoy, he sent the large rounds on a deadly path. The bullets ripped through a truck. Men spilled out the back. Rose flew the length of the convoy as Long Shot riddled each vehicle with a steady stream. The rounds were wasted against tanks, but he fired at the lead one who was attempting to draw a bead on the truck if only to distract the gunner.

The truck was still ten yards short of more solid traction. They were an easy target. The Black Hawk was taking fire now from the troops. The lead Humvee turned down the road toward the truck.

Rose swung the helo low and into the path of the tank's barrel. Then flashed away and went broadside as Long Shot fired at the tank. The barrel changed targets, swinging toward the Black Hawk as she had intended. It bought the truck time.

The small arms fire was beginning to find their marks. Rose waited another instant, then lifted and banked right as the big gun fired. The round sailed past ten yards to the left. The turret moved quickly under experienced hands and toward the helo.

Rose swung in broadside to the Humvee as it turned down the road and barreled toward the truck. It slowed, and six armed soldiers emptied from the doors. Long Shot scattered them, dropping two and sending the others seeking shelter at the side of the Humvee.

Moore was at the back of the truck, adding his firepower to the attack. He had little cover though and was forced back by return fire.

Back at the road, another tank pulled in front of the first. Men were running toward them, spread out across the grounds of the airfield. They were about to be assaulted, and they were all easy targets.

To time the tanks rounds, Rose bounced and swayed, not giving the tank anything to lock onto.

In the distance, Weatherman craned to watch the action wishing he had chosen to ride in the other Black Hawk. He noticed one tank's barrel was high while the other dropped. They were going to fire together at both targets. "Rose," he said, trying to sound calm.

"The second barrel needs to stop moving before they'll fire." Another two seconds passed and she said, "Now!" Instead of shooting upward, she dove. The tanks fired at the same time. The one aiming at the Black Hawk missed. The tank shooting at the truck hit, but the short distance of the shot and the thin metal of the side walls caused the round to pass through, detonating only after striking the second sidewall. Though the truck did not explode, it lifted, banged down, and rocked with such violence it appeared it would tip. Moore was on the ground, stunned by the blast. The soldiers seeing him down, advanced. Rose swept toward them and this time, Long Shot did not let up until they were all down.

Syn Li kept the tires spinning, and when they stopped bouncing caught traction and began to gain ground. The front tires reached solid purchase and gathered speed. As it turned down the road, they could see Money running along the side, spraying a fire extinguisher at the flames. Moore got to his feet and ran as shots from those who reached the hangar began peppering the ground around them. He loped back to the truck, limping. Money tossed the empty canister and raced for the Humvee.

As the tanks lined up another salvo, the van came racing directly at the tanks from the east. With their focus directed at the helo and the truck, they did not see the approach. It swung in front of the first tank, and Jerome leaned out the passenger window. He tossed something on the tank's deck and Sarge pulled forward. Jerome repeated the toss at the second tank, then they made a wide turn and raced back the direction they came as small arms fire chased them.

The explosions rocked the tanks though didn't appear to do any damage. The main benefit of the close blast was startling the gunners, who both hesitated from sending their next rounds downrange. By then, the truck was barreling down the road with the Humvee right behind. As the road curved behind trees, the next round was fired from the tanks. It exploded against a tree tearing the top third of the trunk into the air in a shower of splinters that fell over both vehicles startling the drivers and almost resulting in a collision.

Rose knew another shell was coming and pushed the helo to its limits straining for the cover of the trees. They had been extremely lucky so far, though luck had a way of running out.

She heard the salvo release and dove for the space beyond the trees. The round hit the top of a tree and exploded large chunks of wood into the tail rotor sending the Black Hawk into a sudden spin. Unsure if she could control it and already close to the ground, she bled off speed and yelled, "Brace." The helo hit hard on its landing wheels, bounced, hit bounced, and kept spinning.

Weatherman witnessed the hard landing and turned to the mechanic. "Turn around. Now!"

The frightened man did as ordered. They flew back low, passing between trees on both sides of the road and a mere ten feet above the truck.

"I don't know if I can fix that until I see the damage," the mechanic stuttered.

"I doubt we have the time. Land well to the side so we can use the trees for cover. We'll load everyone onboard."

They landed hard and fast. The mechanic said, "I can see from here the tail rotor is damaged. It will be difficult to fly unless we can straighten the blades."

As Weatherman gave instructions, he saw Long Shot sprint toward the trees nearest the road, rifle in hand. Ellie was at the machine gun. "Keep it running and ready to take off." He got out and raced for the downed Black Hawk. Rose was out of the pilot's seat, pulling Astronaut toward the side. Weatherman arrived and hauled Astronaut up and out. "Rose, gather anything you can carry and take over the other helo." He tossed Astronaut over his shoulder and hurried to the helo.

Shots came from the woods. Long Shot had engaged the enemy troops. He'd keep them back for as long as he was able, but there were too many and no amount of skill was going to stop the tanks. Weatherman could already hear the rumble of their tracks over the blacktop road.

Sarge came speeding down the road from the south. He spied the downed helo and veered across the grass, bringing the van around. Jerome jumped out and climbed inside, taking over the machine gun. "Help Rose collect whatever you can." Ellie gave him a vehement look but did as he instructed.

Rose jumped out with an arm full of weapons and ran to the second Black Hawk. Ellie did the same, but Jerome stopped her. "Put it in the van," he shouted. "It's closer."

Weatherman returned as Jerome fired toward the road at enemy soldiers.

The tanks were close. "Jerome," he said over the chatter of the gun. "Go now, or you won't get away. We'll meet down the road." Long Shot, who had been keeping the troops from advancing with a steady stream of deadly accurate fire, was on the run waving his arms frantically to go.

Jerome jumped into the Humvee with Ellie still in the back, depositing the load she carried over. Money had the vehicle moving fast. It cut a long diagonal path across the field toward the road. Weatherman took up the gun and covered Long Shot as he sprinted past, moving toward the second Black Hawk.

Weatherman waited until he was halfway there before grabbing a bag of something from the floor and running after him. The tank had cleared the tree line and was swinging the turret in the helo's direction. The round was fired. The Black Hawk behind him exploded, sending shards of debris in all directions. The concussion knocked Weatherman off stride. He tumbled, rolled, and was back on his feet in an instant

He was barely through the door before Rose was airborne. She kept low and fast banking left to use the trees as cover if possible. They cleared the trees by a narrow margin. Once past the trees, she dove beneath the treetops and then changed to a more southern course.

Chapter Thirty-Eight

Two miles further, Rose picked up the road. She hovered until they caught sight of the van and the Humvee. Jerome stuck an arm out the window and waved. Rose stayed with them until they hit highway forty-one south. They did not see any sign of the truck moving or ditched.

Rose turned back to locate the truck. If they needed help, they didn't want to abandon them, even though that's what Moore and his partner appeared to have done.

"Maybe the truck broke down someplace," Weatherman said.

"Maybe," was all Rose said. Her tone suggested she didn't believe that was the case.

They retraced their route until they spotted the enemy vehicles searching for them, then Rose tried alternate routes Moore might have taken. Unless they were in deep hiding, the truck had left the area.

"He knows where we're going. Right?"

"Supposedly," Rose said.

"You don't trust Moore?"

She gave him a sideways glance. "You don't either, so don't question me."

Long Shot slid forward. "You have to admit there is something off about the guy."

"Maybe, but there's nothing we can do for them if we can't find them. The options are they broke down and are hiding, they're on an alternate route, or Moore is bugging out. First way, they stay hidden, and we don't see them again. Second way, they hook up with us down the road. He doesn't have a radio, so it may be guesswork on his part as to where we are. Third way, if Moore's running, we let him go. I think we move on." Weatherman looked from Rose to Long Shot for agreement.

Long Shot nodded. "Nothing we can do now. If he is in trouble though, he can't call for help."

Rose was a long time giving her approval. "I may not trust him, but I don't like leaving him behind."

"Agreed," said Weatherman. "We can stay and keep looking."

Rose let out a prolonged breath. "No. We go and trust he's on track."

"Let's find the others," said Weatherman.

Twenty minutes later, they caught sight of the van and Humvee still on forty-one. They stayed with them until they were north of Indianapolis. Sarge had plotted a course along smaller highways staying off the interstates.

"We need to decide what to do," Weatherman said.

"They're undermanned now," Long Shot said.

"Do either of you know Voodoo?"

Rose shook her head, still upset about leaving Money behind.

"Not me," said Long Shot.

"What about Monster?"

Neither knew him either.

"Well, that creates a dilemma," Weatherman said.

"Maybe we all need to go together and do one mission," said Long Shot.

"It will be slower, but it's the only option. Signal the van that we're setting down."

"Hold on that," Ellie said from the back seat. She had been scanning both sides of the helo with glasses, searching for threats. "I see the truck. It's to our left about, oh, I can't estimate distances. Miles."

Rose banked left and Long Shot took the binoculars. "She's got them. Make it ten miles out driving down that expressway that's right in front of us now."

Weatherman and Rose leaned forward as if the extra few inches helped their view that much more. "Got them," said Rose with a note of excitement in her voice. As they skirted the city, Rose flew ahead, settled in front of the truck, and waggled the helo side to side, then banked west. She hovered over an interchange and waited for the truck. The top back of the passenger side was blackened and had a four-foot diameter hole. They had been lucky.

When the truck reached the junction, Syn Li made the turn. Rose guided them across I-70 until they reached I-64. There they fell in behind the Humvee.

Relieved the team was back together, she faced Weatherman. "Maybe I was wrong."

"Maybe we all were," Long Shot said.

Weatherman said, "Maybe."

Rose lowered in front of the van and waggled again, this time to signal goodbye. Then she lifted off and set course for Texas.

Jerome watched them go until they were a dot that blinked out.

"Guess we're on our own now," Sarge said.

"You still okay with this?"

"Hell, ain't got nothing better to do."

"You mean than save the country?"

"Been doing that my whole life. What's another crisis to overcome?"

Jerome laughed. "Odds are a little different this time. Not to mention we're fighting our military in our own country."

"I do hate killing our own people, especially if they been led astray. Maybe this Money fellow can convince a bunch of them the cause they're backing is the wrong one. If we get the military on our side, the instigators won't have anyone to fight for them. We can change things back, makes things right."

"Sarge, this can never be made right. Look how many lives have been sacrificed. Too many people have died for this ever to go back. We can only hope to move forward, grow, and make sure nothing like this can ever happen again."

They were silent for a long time. Then Sarge said, "Couldn't ask for a better person to bring about that change than you."

"I appreciate that, Sarge, but it's going to take a whole lot of people like both of us to bring about the necessary changes." It's going to take an army, he thought. "We're just the beginning."

The story continues in Random Survival: The Road Book 6 Voodoo and Shaman.

ABOUT THE AUTHOR

Ray Wenck taught elementary school for 36 years. He was also the chef/owner of DeSimone's Italian restaurant for more than 25 years. After retiring he became a lead cook for Hollywood Casinos and then the kitchen manager for the Toledo Mud Hens AAA baseball team. Now he spends most of his time writing, doing book tours and meeting old and new fans and friends around the country.

Ray is the author of forty-six novels including the Amazon Top 20 post-apocalyptic, Random Survival series, the paranormal thriller, Reclamation, the mystery/suspense Danny Roth series and the ever popular choose your own adventure, Pick-A-Path: Apocalypse. A list of his other novels can be viewed at raywenck.com.

His hobbies include reading, hiking, cooking, baseball and playing the harmonica with any band brave enough to allow him to sit in.

You can find his books all your favorite sites.

You can reach Ray or sign up for his newsletter at raywenck.com or authorraywenck on Facebook

For a free book, visit raywenck.com and sign up for the newsletter.

Other Titles

Random Survival Series
Random Survival
The Long Search for Home
The Endless Struggle
A Journey to Normal
Then There'll Be None
In Defense of Home
A Life Worth Dying For

Danny Roth Series
Teammates
Teamwork
Home Team
Stealing Home
Group Therapy
Double Play
Playing Through Errors
Pitch Count

The Dead Series
Tower of the Dead
Island of the Dead
Escaping the Dead

Pick-A-Path Series
Pick-A-Path: Apocalypse 1
Pick-A-Path: Apocalypse 2
Pick-A-Path: Apocalypse 3

Stand Alone Titles
Warriors of the Court
Live to Die Again
The Eliminator
Reclamation
Dimensions
Ghost of a Chance
Mischief Magic
Twins In Time
When the Cheering Stops

Short Stories
The Con   Short Stop-A Danny Roth short
Super Me   Super Me, Too

Co-authored with Jason J. Nugent
Escape: The Seam Travelers Book 1
Capture: The Seam Travelers Book 2
Conquest: The Seam Travelers Book 3

The Historian Series

The Historian: Life Before and After

The Historian: The Wilds

The Historian: Invasion

Jeremy Kline

The Invisible Village

The Lost Tribe

Bridgett Conroy Series

A Second Chance at Death

Traveling Trouble

Ray Wenck

Ray Wenck

Made in the USA
Monee, IL
10 June 2023